“Look at me, Ste[illegible]
“Really look at m[illegible] pressed.

W9-CBE-735

Stephanie had already looked. Several times! And yes, he was obviously thinner, gaunter, grimmer than he had been six months ago, but as far as she was concerned, none of that detracted from the fact that he was a compellingly handsome man.

“What am I looking for?”

Jordan gave an impatient snort. “What was it you called me earlier? A cripple, wasn’t it?”

She gasped at the bitterness in his tone. “No, what I actually said was that *you* obviously believe yourself to be a cripple,” she corrected firmly.

“Maybe because that’s what I am?” he said harshly. “I certainly don’t want any woman to be with me just because she feels sorry for me.”

“That’s ridiculous—”

“This from the woman who just refused me?” he taunted.

Stephanie rolled her eyes. “We both know you weren’t being serious.”

“Do we?”

THE SCANDALOUS ST. CLAIRES

Three arrogant aristocrats—ready to marry!

Don't miss any of Carole Mortimer's fabulous trilogy:

April—THE RETURN OF THE RENEGADE
May—THE RELUCTANT DUKE
June—TAMING THE LAST ST. CLAIRE

And read where it all began—
with *The Notorious St. Claires* in Regency England!

Only in Harlequin® Historical

Carole Mortimer

THE RETURN OF THE RENEGADE

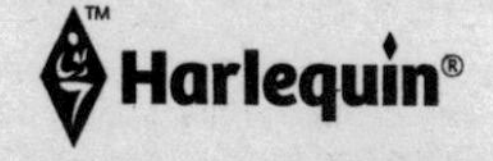

TORONTO NEW YORK LONDON
AMSTERDAM PARIS SYDNEY HAMBURG
STOCKHOLM ATHENS TOKYO MILAN MADRID
PRAGUE WARSAW BUDAPEST AUCKLAND

If you purchased this book without a cover you should be aware that this book is stolen property. It was reported as "unsold and destroyed" to the publisher, and neither the author nor the publisher has received any payment for this "stripped book."

Recycling programs for this product may not exist in your area.

ISBN-13: 978-0-373-12982-9

THE RETURN OF THE RENEGADE

Previously published in the U.K. as
JORDAN ST CLAIRE: DARK AND DANGEROUS

First North American Publication 2011

Copyright © 2011 by Carole Mortimer

All rights reserved. Except for use in any review, the reproduction or utilization of this work in whole or in part in any form by any electronic, mechanical or other means, now known or hereafter invented, including xerography, photocopying and recording, or in any information storage or retrieval system, is forbidden without the written permission of the publisher, Harlequin Enterprises Limited, 225 Duncan Mill Road, Don Mills, Ontario, Canada M3B 3K9.

This is a work of fiction. Names, characters, places and incidents are either the product of the author's imagination or are used fictitiously, and any resemblance to actual persons, living or dead, business establishments, events or locales is entirely coincidental.

This edition published by arrangement with Harlequin Books S.A.

For questions and comments about the quality of this book please contact us at Customer_eCare@Harlequin.ca.

® and TM are trademarks of the publisher. Trademarks indicated with ® are registered in the United States Patent and Trademark Office, the Canadian Trade Marks Office and in other countries.

www.eHarlequin.com

Printed in U.S.A.

THE RETURN OF THE RENEGADE

PROLOGUE

'I THINK I should warn you, Miss McKinley—at the moment my brother is behaving like an arrogant lout!'

Must run in the family, Stephanie thought wryly as she looked across at Lucan St Claire, who was sitting behind his desk in the London office of the St Claire Corporation. Tall, dark, and aristocratically handsome, with a remoteness that bordered on cold, he wasn't loutish at all—but this man had to be the epitome of arrogant!

The fact that he showed absolutely no interest in her as a woman might have something to do with Stephanie's unkind thoughts—but, hey, a girl could dream of being hotly pursued by a mega-rich, tall, dark and handsome man, couldn't she? That Lucan St Claire had more money than some small countries, and reportedly only dated leggy blondes—as opposed to women like Stephanie, with her average height and flame-red hair—probably had something to do with his lack of interest. Also, if that weren't enough strikes against her, she was merely the self-employed physiotherapist this man intended hiring—she hoped—to aid his younger brother's recuperation.

She steadily returned the piercing darkness of his

gaze. 'Most people in pain tend to become…a little aggressive in their behaviour, Mr St Claire.'

The sculptured lips curved in a humourless smile. 'I believe you will find that Jordan's a *lot* aggressive.'

Stephanie mentally sifted through the relevant facts she already had on the man who was to be her next patient. On a personal level, she knew Jordan St Claire was thirty-four, and the youngest of three brothers. Medically, she knew Jordan had been involved in some sort of accident six months ago, resulting in his having broken almost every bone down the right side of his body. Numerous operations later, his mobility still impaired, the man had apparently retreated from the world by moving to a house in the English countryside, no doubt with the intention of licking his wounds in private.

So far Stephanie found nothing unusual about his behaviour. 'I'm sure that it's nothing I haven't dealt with in other patients, Mr St Claire,' she said confidently.

Lucan St Claire leant his elbows on the leather-topped desk to look at her above steepled fingers. 'What I'm trying to explain is that Jordan may be…less than enthusiastic, shall we say?…even at the mere thought of having yet another physiotherapist working with him.'

As Stephanie had never thought of herself as 'yet another physiotherapist', she found the remark less than flattering. She was proud of the success she had made of her private practice these past three years. A success that had resulted in almost all her clients coming as referrals from doctors or other satisfied ex-patients.

From what Stephanie had read in the medical file that now sat on top of Lucan St Claire's desk—a confidential file that she was sure he shouldn't even have had access to, let alone a copy of—the surgeons had done their work, and now it was up to Jordan St Claire to do the rest. Something he obviously seemed less than inclined to do…

Her eyes narrowed as she studied the aristocratically haughty face opposite her own. 'What is it you aren't telling me, Mr St Claire?' she finally prompted slowly.

He gave a brief appreciative smile. 'I can see that your professional reputation for straight talking is well earned.'

Stephanie was well aware that her brisk manner, along with her no-nonsense appearance—her long red hair was secured in a thick braid down her spine, and there was only a light brush of mascara on the long dark lashes that surrounded cool green eyes—invariably gave the impression she was less than emotionally engaged. It wasn't true, of course, but inwardly empathising with her patients was one thing, and allowing them to *see* that empathy something else entirely.

As for her professional reputation…

Thank goodness Lucan St Claire didn't give any indication that he had heard any of the rumours concerning Rosalind Newman's recent accusation—that Stephanie had been involved in an affair with her husband Richard whilst acting as his physiotherapist. If he had, then she doubted he would even be thinking of engaging her.

'I've never seen any point in being less than truthful.' She shrugged. 'Especially when it involves my patients.'

Lucan nodded in agreement. 'Jordan wouldn't accept anything less.' He sat back in his black leather chair.

'And…?' Stephanie pierced him with shrewd green eyes. If she was going to work with this man's brother then she needed to know everything there was to know about him—and not just his medical background.

He gave a heavy sigh. 'And Jordan has absolutely no idea about my intention of engaging you.'

Stephanie had already had a suspicion that might be the case. It made her job more difficult, of course, if the patient was hostile towards her before she had even begun working with him, but she had worked with difficult patients before. In fact most of Stephanie's patients were difficult; her reputation for being able to deal with 'uncooperative' patients was the reason there had been no shortage of work since she had opened her small clinic.

'Can I take it from that remark it's your intention to present him with a *fait accompli*?'

He grimaced. 'Either way, he's as likely to tell you to go away—impolitely—as he is to let you anywhere near him.'

Stephanie pursed her lips. 'If you engaged me we would just have to make it impossible for him to tell me to go away—impolitely or otherwise. I believe you said that the house where he's staying in Gloucestershire is actually owned by you?'

Lucan eyed her warily. 'It's part of an estate owned by the St Claire Corporation, yes.'

'Then as the head of that corporation you obviously have the right to say who does and does not stay there.' Her gaze was very direct.

He looked at her appreciatively, those dark eyes gleaming with hard humour. 'You wouldn't have a problem just turning up there and facing the consequences?'

'If my patient leaves me with no other choice, no,' she assured him bluntly.

He smiled slowly. 'I do believe that Jordan may have more than met his match in you!'

Stephanie brightened. 'You've decided to engage me to work with your brother?'

'Working *with* Jordan might be an exaggeration,' Lucan drawled ruefully. 'He's been very vocal in not wanting anyone else "poking and prodding" him about, as if he's a specimen in a jar.'

'I never poke or prod, Mr St Claire,' Stephanie said dryly, her interest in the case deepening as she considered the hard work ahead of her. 'I can begin next week, if that would suit you?' She had absolutely no intention of allowing this man to even guess how relieved she felt at the thought of getting out of London for a while.

Away from Rosalind Newman's nasty—and totally untrue—accusations that Stephanie had had an affair with her husband…

'Very much so.' He looked relieved that nothing he had told her about his brother seemed to have succeeded in deterring her.

Stephanie understood that relief only too well—knew that very often a patient's inability to deal with their illness affected close family as much as it did them. Sometimes more so. And, for all that Lucan St Claire was known for his coldness and arrogance, he obviously loved his brother very much.

'I will need a key to the house where he's staying, and directions on how to get there,' she said. 'What happens next you may safely leave to me.'

Jordan St Claire didn't know it yet, but the immovable object was about to meet the unstoppable force!

CHAPTER ONE

'WHO the hell are *you*? And what are you doing in my kitchen?'

Stephanie had arrived at the gatehouse of Mulberry Hall an hour or so ago, and had rung the bell and knocked on the door before deciding that either Jordan St Claire wasn't in or he was just refusing to answer. Either way, it left her with no choice but to let herself in with the key Lucan St Claire had given her. Once she had walked into the kitchen and seen the mess there she hadn't bothered going any further. The dirty plates and untidiness were a complete affront to her inborn need for order and cleanliness. She doubted Jordan had bothered to wash a single cup or plate since his arrival here a month ago!

'*This* is a kitchen?' She continued to collect up the dirty crockery that seemed to litter every surface, before dropping it gingerly into the sink full of hot, soapy water. 'I thought it was a laboratory for growing bacterial cultures!' She turned, her gaze very direct as she raised derisive dark brows at the unkempt man who stood in the doorway, glaring at her so accusingly.

Only to feel the need to steady herself by leaning against one of the kitchen cabinets as she instantly recognised him. Despite the untidy overlong dark hair, the several days' growth of beard on the sculptured square jaw, and the way the black T-shirt and faded blue jeans hung slightly loose on his large frame, there was no mistaking his identity.

It took every ounce of Stephanie's usual calm collectedness to keep her expression coolly mocking as she found herself looking not at Jordan St Claire but at the world-famous actor Jordan Simpson!

Admittedly, the shaggy dark hair and the five o'clock shadow that looked more like an eleven o'clock one managed to disguise most of his handsome features—which was perhaps the intention. But there was no mistaking those mesmerising amber-gold eyes. Reviewers' descriptions of the colour of those eyes differed from molten gold to amber to cinnamon-brown—but, whatever the colour, the descriptions were always preceded by the word *mesmerising*!

As a fan of the English actor, who had taken Hollywood by storm ten years ago when, as a relative unknown, he had been given the starring role in a film that had been an instant box office hit, Stephanie knew exactly who he was. She should do, when she had seen every film this man had ever made—twenty or so to date. A couple of them had even resulted in him winning Oscars for his stunning performances, and she would have recognised those chiselled features in the dark. In her many fantasies involving this man it had always been in the dark…

Added to which, she knew Jordan Simpson had fallen from the top of a building six months ago, whilst on the set of his last film. The newspapers had been full of sensational speculation at the time, hinting that Jordan had been severely disfigured. That he might never walk again. That he might never work again.

No doubt about it, Stephanie accepted, as her heart continued to beat rapidly and her cheeks started to feel hot, he might be walking with the aid of a cane, but the man in front of her really *was* the incredibly handsome actor she had obsessed over for years. A little fact that Lucan St Claire had forgotten to mention to her the previous week, she thought with annoyance. She'd rather have been forewarned!

'Very funny!' Jordan rasped in response to her remark about the kitchen. He stood in the doorway, leaning heavily on the ebony cane he had necessarily to carry around with him everywhere nowadays if he didn't want to end up falling flat on his face. 'That still doesn't tell me who you are or how you got in.'

Jordan had been in an exhausted sleep, lying on the bed that had been brought down to the dining room because he could no longer walk up the stairs, when he'd heard the sound of someone moving about in the kitchen. His first thought had been that it was a burglar, but intruders didn't usually hang around long enough to wash the dishes!

'I have a key.' The redhead shrugged.

His eyes narrowed. 'Given to you by whom, exactly?'

A slight indrawn breath and then another shrug. 'Your brother Lucan.'

Jordan's glare turned to a scowl. 'If my interfering brother sent you here to act as housekeeper, then I think you should know I don't need one.'

'All evidence is to the contrary,' the redhead drawled, and she turned her back on him to once again move efficiently about the kitchen, collecting up yet more dirty plates and stacking them on the draining board. Giving Jordan's narrowed gaze every opportunity to notice how a short white T-shirt clung to the firmness of her breasts and flat stomach, ending a couple of inches short of the low-slung jeans that moulded to narrow hips and the perfect curve of her bottom.

Great—the only part of his body that didn't already ache from his injuries was now engorged, throbbing and ached like hell!

It was the first time Jordan had felt the least bit of sexual interest in a woman since the accident six months ago—but, considering the pitiful condition the rest of his body was in, it wasn't an interest he particularly welcomed now. 'Most of that stuff will go into the dishwasher, you know,' he muttered resentfully as the redhead began to wash the dishes already in the soapy water in the sink.

'They *could* have gone in the dishwasher after they were first used,' she corrected without turning. 'Now they need to be soaked first.'

'Implying that I'm a slob?'

'Oh, it wasn't an implication,' she commented pertly.

'It may have escaped your notice, but I'm slightly impaired here!' Jordan defended angrily; he didn't have much of an appetite nowadays anyway, but on the occasions he did feel hungry his hip and leg ached so much by the time he had finished preparing the food and eating it that he didn't feel up to doing the dishes.

The redhead stopped washing up to slowly turn and look at him with wide green eyes. 'Wow.' She gave a rueful shake of her head. 'I have to admit I didn't expect you to play the "I'm crippled" card right off the bat!'

Jordan drew in a harsh, disbelieving breath even as his fingers tightened about his cane until the knuckles showed white. '*What* did you just say?'

Stephanie's gaze continued to calmly meet Jordan's fierce amber eyes even as she quickly registered the way his already pale cheeks had taken on a grey tinge, along with the resentful stiffening of a body that obviously showed the signs of being ravaged by pain and illness.

Normally a complete professional when it came to her job, Stephanie was finding it difficult to deal with Jordan's dark and sensual good-looks with her usual detachment. In fact, she had deliberately not looked at him for some minutes in an effort to regain her equilibrium! Usually level-headed when it came to men, Stephanie had dragged her reluctant sister along to see every film Jordan Simpson had ever made, just so that she could sit in the impersonal darkness of the cinema and drool over the big screen image of him before she was later able to buy the film on DVD and drool over him in private. Her sister Joey was just going to fall over laughing when she learnt who Stephanie had taken on as her patient!

Her expression remained outwardly cool as she inwardly acknowledged that thankfully the sexy and ruggedly handsome actor was barely recognisable in the gaunt and pale man in front of her. Except for those eyes!

'I'm sorry. I thought that was how you now thought of yourself? As a cripple,' she said evenly.

Those eyes glittered a dangerous gold. 'Forget who you are and what you're doing here, and just get the hell out of my home!' he ordered furiously.

'I don't think so.'

He frowned fiercely at the calmness of her reply. 'You don't?'

Stephanie smiled unconcernedly in the face of the

fury she could see he was trying so hard to restrain. 'This is your brother's home, not yours, and the fact that Lucan gave me a key to get in shows he has no problem with me being here.'

Jordan drew in a harsh breath. '*I* have a problem with you being here.'

She smiled slightly. 'Unfortunately for you, you aren't the one paying the bills.'

'I don't need a damned housekeeper!' he repeated, frustrated.

'As I said, that's questionable,' Stephanie teased lightly as she moved to dry her hands on a towel that also looked as if it needed to come face to face with some hot soapy water—or, more preferably, disinfectant! 'Stephanie McKinley.' She thrust out the dry hand. 'And I'm not a housekeeper.'

A hand Jordan deliberately chose to ignore, breathing deeply as he looked down at her from between narrowed lids. Probably aged in her mid to late twenties, the woman had incredibly long, dark lashes fringing eyes of deep green, and the freckles that usually accompanied hair as red as hers were a light dusting across her small uptilted nose. Her lips were full, the bottom one slightly more so than the top, above a pointed and determined chin. She also had one very sexy body beneath the casual white T-shirt and denims, and—as he was now all too well aware—a tongue like a viper!

No one—not even his two brothers—had dared to talk to Jordan these last few months in the way Stephanie McKinley just had…

'How do you know Lucan?' Jordan probed suddenly.

'I don't.' With a shrug, the woman allowed her hand to fall back to her side. 'At least, not in the way I think you're implying I might.' She gave him another mocking glance.

Jordan had been standing for longer than he usually did, and as a result his hip was starting to ache. Badly. A definite strain on his already short temper! 'Is paying a woman to go to bed with me Lucan's idea of a joke?'

Stephanie smiled in the face of the deliberate insult—at the same time as she wryly wondered whether the coldly remote man she had met the previous week even had a sense of humour! 'Do I *look* like a woman men pay to go to bed with them?'

'How the hell should I know?' Jordan scorned.

'Implying you don't usually need to pay a woman to go to bed with you?' That was something she was already well aware of—Jordan Simpson had trouble keeping women out of his bed rather than the opposite!

'Not usually, no,' he ground out.

Stephanie realised that he was deliberately trying to unnerve and embarrass her with the intimacy of this conversation. He was succeeding, too—which wasn't a good thing in the circumstances.

She raised an eyebrow. 'I assure you I would have absolutely no interest in going to bed with a man who is so full of self-pity that he's not only shut himself off from his family but the rest of the world, too.'

Jordan's face darkened ominously. 'What the hell would *you* know about it?' he snarled viciously. 'I don't see *you* suffering pitying looks every time you so much as go outside, as you stumble about with the aid of a cane just so that you don't completely embarrass yourself by falling flat on your backside!'

Stephanie hesitated slightly before answering. 'Not any more, no…'

Those golden eyes narrowed to dark slits. 'What exactly does *that* mean?'

Stephanie calmly met that furiously glittering gaze. 'It means that when I was ten years old I was involved in a car crash that left me confined to a wheelchair for two years. I couldn't walk at all for all of that time, not even to "stumble about with the aid of a cane". You, on the other hand, still have mobility in both your legs, which is why you won't be receiving any of those pitying looks from me that you seem to find so offensive from the rest of humanity!'

Ordinarily Stephanie didn't tell her patients of her own years spent in a wheelchair. She saw no reason why she needed to, and wouldn't have done so now, either, if the challenge in Jordan's tone hadn't touched on a raw nerve.

'You were lucky enough to get up and walk so now you think anyone else who finds themselves in the same position should do the same?' he said.

'So you've had the bad luck to receive injuries that have left you less than your previously robust and healthy self. Either live with it, or fight it, but don't hide yourself away here, feeling sorry for yourself.' She was breathing hard in her agitation.

Jordan looked down at her with sudden comprehension. 'If Lucan didn't send you here to go to bed with me, then who the hell *are* you? Yet another doctor? Or perhaps my arrogant big brother now thinks I'm in need of a shrink?' His top lip turned back contemptuously.

Stephanie McKinley quirked dark brows. 'I had the impression from reading your medical notes that your skull escaped injury when you fell?'

'It did,' he bit out tightly.

She raised auburn brows. 'Do *you* think you're in need of a psychiatrist?'

He scowled darkly. 'I'm not playing this game with you, Miss McKinley.'

'I assure you I don't consider this a game, Mr Simpson—'

'You know who I am?' Jordan interjected.

'Well, of *course* I know who you are.' Irritation creased the smooth creaminess of her brow. 'You're a household name. Obviously you're feeling less than your usual…suave and charming self,' she concluded tactfully, 'but you're still *you*.'

Was he? Sometimes Jordan wondered. Until six months ago he had enjoyed his life. Living in California. Doing the work he loved to do. 'Suave and charming' enough to be able to go to bed with any woman who took his interest. Since the accident all that had changed. *He* had changed.

'In that case, Miss McKinley, what I need is for someone to find a screenplay that calls for a male lead who limps! Know of any?' Jordan growled his frustration as he moved away from her, favouring his right side as usual, as the damaged muscle and bones in his hip and leg protested at the movement. Hell, he hurt no matter if he moved or not!

'Not offhand, no,' the redhead said tartly. 'And you wouldn't need one if you concentrated your energies on getting back the full use of that leg instead of wallowing in self-pity.'

'Damn it to hell!' Jordan gave a groan of disgust, his eyes lifting to the heavens in supplication. 'You're another sadistic physiotherapist, aren't you? Come to pound and massage until I can't stand the pain any longer.' It was a statement, not a question; Jordan had

had one physiotherapist or another working on his leg and hip for weeks, months, since the surgeon had finished putting his shattered bones back together. None of them had succeeded in doing more than sending him to hell and back.

'The fact that the leg still hurts could be a positive thing, not a negative one,' Stephanie McKinley retorted.

'I'll be sure to think of that at two o'clock in the morning, when I can't sleep because the pain is driving me insane!'

When Lucan St Claire had warned Stephanie that his brother was 'a *lot* aggressive', he had forgotten to add that he was also stubborn and unreasonable! 'In this case pain could be a good thing—it could mean the muscles are regenerating,' she explained patiently.

'Or it could mean that they're dying!'

'Well, yes…' No point in trying to deceive him concerning that possibility. 'I'll be able to tell you more once I've worked with it—'

'The only part of my body I would be remotely interested in having any woman work with is a couple of inches higher than my thigh!' he shot back wickedly.

There was no way, complete professional or not, Stephanie could have prevented the heated flush that now coloured her cheeks. Or the way her gaze moved instinctively down to the area in question. That particular part of his anatomy certainly seemed to be working normally, if the hard and lengthy bulge she could see pressing against his jeans was anything to go by!

Jordan St Claire—no, Jordan *Simpson*—was obviously physically aroused. By her.

No, not by her in particular, Stephanie rebuked herself impatiently. She very much doubted that this man had allowed a woman within touching distance since his accident, and after six months of celibacy she was probably just the first reasonably attractive female he had seen in a while—consequently he would have been aroused by a nun, as long as she had a pulse and breasts!

'If you're trying to embarrass me, Mr Simpson—'

'Then I've succeeded.' He eyed her flushed cheeks triumphantly.

'Perhaps,' she allowed briskly. 'Does knowing that make you feel good?' She eyed him speculatively as he gave a hard and unapologetic grin. A slow and sexy grin that reminded her all too forcibly that this man was the actor she had lusted after for years.

Oh, help!

He gave a casual shrug. 'It doesn't matter whether it did or it didn't. I intend to forget you even exist as soon as you've walked out the door.'

This time it was Stephanie's turn to smile slowly. 'You're an altogether arrogant family, aren't you?'

Jordan gave a huff of laughter. 'How many of us have you met?'

Stephanie blinked. 'Just Lucan and you…'

'And you think *we're* arrogant?' He snorted. 'Believe me, you don't know what arrogance is until you've met Gideon.'

'Your twin?'

That golden gaze sharpened. 'You seem to know a lot about me.'

She shrugged. 'I believe it's public knowledge that Jordan Simpson has a twin brother.'

He grimaced. 'Gideon and I are only fraternal twins, not identical ones.'

Thank goodness for that! Stephanie wasn't sure the

world—or she—could stand there being two men in the world with Jordan's devastating good-looks.

She had yet to decide whether or not this man posed a problem as regarded her working with him—other than the need she felt every time she so much as looked at him to rip his clothes off and jump into bed with him, of course. But surely that was normal? Hundreds—no, *thousands* of women must feel the same way about the actor Jordan Simpson. Except none of those women were supposed to act the complete professional and treat this man like any other patient—which he most certainly wasn't to Stephanie!

She gave a weary sigh as she pushed back some loose tendrils of hair that had escaped the plait down her spine. 'Look, Mr Simpson, I've had a long drive up here from London, and on top of that I could do with something to eat, so do you think we could call a truce to this argument long enough for me to cook us some dinner?'

Jordan's eyes narrowed contemplatively. On the one hand he wanted this woman gone from here, but on the other the mention of food had reminded him that he was hungry—a side-effect of those damned sleeping pills he had to take in order to get any rest at all. 'That depends,' he finally murmured slowly.

Deep green eyes looked across at him suspiciously. 'On what?'

'On whether or not you can actually cook, of course,' Jordan drawled. 'Put another plate of baked beans on toast in front of me and I may just throw it at you!' He had been living off something on toast since he'd moved here a month ago, in too much pain and lacking the appetite to bother to cook anything else.

Lucan had gone to the trouble of sending this woman

here, but Jordan had no intention of even allowing her to look at his injuries. Sex didn't appear to be on her agenda either. So she might as well make herself useful in some other way—before Jordan went ahead and threw her out anyway!

'I think I can do better than that,' Stephanie McKinley told him. 'I wasn't sure what the situation was for having groceries delivered, so I brought some things with me,' she continued brightly. 'I'll just go out to the car and get them.' She collected her black jacket from the back of one of the kitchen chairs and slipped it on, releasing her braid from the collar before moving towards the door. 'I hope you like steak?'

Just the mention of red meat was enough to make Jordan's mouth water. 'No doubt I could cope,' he said gruffly.

Stephanie was smiling slightly to herself as she went out to her car. He was allowing her to stay long enough to cook dinner, at least. Unsurprising, when she knew from the dirty plates she had collected up earlier that Jordan hadn't been exaggerating about the amount of baked beans on toast he had eaten since coming here. What happened after Stephanie had fed him was still in question, of course; she wasn't fooled for a moment by his sudden acquiescence in allowing her to cook dinner for them both.

She was going to have dinner with Jordan Simpson!

Admittedly he was a Jordan Simpson much changed from the charming, sensual man she had read about so much in the newspapers over the years. Or the one she had gazed at so longingly on the big and small screen, but still…

Stephanie had barely had time to open her car door when she heard her mobile ringing. Bending down to pick it up from where it lay on the passenger seat, she checked the number of the caller. 'Joey?' she breathed thankfully as she pressed the receiver to her ear and took her sister's call. 'I'm so glad you rang! I think I might be in trouble. *Big* trouble!'

CHAPTER TWO

'I THOUGHT you had decided to get in your car and leave after all,' Jordan rasped when Stephanie McKinley finally came back into the kitchen, carrying a box of groceries.

She put the box down on the kitchen table before answering him, her face slightly flushed, and even more of that long fiery-red hair having escaped the confining plait. 'I stopped to admire how beautiful the big house looked in the distance, with the sun going down behind it.'

'Mulberry Hall?'

She nodded. 'Is it a hotel, or something?'

'Or something.' Jordan nodded tersely. He had sat down at the kitchen table while he waited for her to return, and stretched his leg out in front of him now as he watched Stephanie take steak, potatoes, asparagus and salad from the box with hands that were long and slender, the nails trimmed capably short. No doubt in readiness for the sadistic pummelling she gave her patients!

'Either it is a hotel or it isn't,' she reasoned with a slight frown as she paused in the unpacking.

'It isn't,' Jordan supplied unhelpfully. The sight of all this fresh food reminded him of just how long it had been since he had last eaten. Yesterday some time, he thought. Maybe.

Besides which, he had absolutely no intention of talking about Mulberry Hall, or its function, with a woman who was going to be gone from here in a few hours.

'Your brother Lucan said this whole estate was owned by the St Claire Corporation.'

Jordan's mouth twisted. 'Did he?'

She raised dark brows. 'If you don't want to talk about it then just say so.'

He shrugged. 'I don't want to talk about it.'

Well, she had definitely asked for that one, Stephanie acknowledged ruefully. 'I was only trying to make polite conversation.'

Jordan looked at her coldly. 'I agreed to let you cook dinner, not talk.'

Stephanie bit back her angry retort as she resumed unpacking the box of groceries. Maybe he would be more amenable after he had eaten? And maybe he wouldn't! she thought dryly.

His medical file had stated that the broken bones in his arm and ribcage had knitted back together well, but the lines of strain grooved beside his mouth and eyes were evidence of the pain he still suffered in the hip and leg that had been fractured and obviously hadn't healed as well. Stephanie's fingers itched to explore that damaged leg and hip, to check for herself what could be done about restoring this man to full mobility.

Or maybe they just itched to touch all six foot four inches of lean, male flesh that was Jordan Simpson…

Her sister had been first incredulous and then amused when Stephanie had explained her dilemma to her, dismissing her misgivings regarding having the actor as her newest patient.

Joey had also reassured Stephanie concerning her worry over her unwilling involvement in the Newmans' divorce. Her lawyer sister had advised Stephanie to 'just get on and do what you do best, sis, and leave me to deal with the Newman situation.'

That the 'Newman situation' even needed dealing with still rankled with Stephanie.

'Could you lay the table while I cook?' she prompted sharply.

His jaw clenched. 'I'm not a complete invalid, damn it.' He gritted very white teeth as he rose awkwardly to his feet before grasping the ebony cane to balance himself.

'It was a request for you to actually lay the table, not a question as to whether or not you're capable of doing it,' she elaborated.

'Of course it was,' he said sarcastically.

Stephanie watched him as he limped across the kitchen to open the cutlery drawer, determinedly keeping her gaze professional. The muscles in his leg were obviously weakened from months of disuse, but that didn't explain the amount of pain he seemed to be suffering. It might be an idea to have someone else look at him—

'What the hell are you looking at?'

Stephanie raised her gaze to find Jordan scowling across the kitchen at her, and the look of savage anger on that handsome face warned her to opt for honesty. 'I was wondering if you should have that leg and hip re-X-rayed.'

'Forget it.' He threw the cutlery noisily back into the drawer before slamming it shut. 'And while you're at it take your food and just get out!' He walked stiffly towards the door that led back into the hallway.

Stephanie frowned her dismay as she realised his obvious intention of leaving. 'What about dinner?'

Those amber eyes were glittering furiously as he turned to glare at her. 'I just lost my appetite.'

'Just because I talked about your leg?'

'Because you talked at *all*,' Jordan told her insultingly. 'Men just shut up and get on with it—whereas women, I've learnt, feel the need to dissect everything.'

'If by that you mean that men prefer to bottle up their anxieties rather than—'

'The only anxiety I have at this moment is *you*!' he cut in viciously, able to feel the nerve pulsing in his tightly clenched jaw. 'A situation that will resolve itself the moment you walk out the door.'

This man really was an immovable object, Stephanie recognised in sheer frustration. Well, two could play at that game! 'I'm not going anywhere,' she told him levelly.

Those glittering amber eyes turned icily cold as his gaze raked over her from head to toe and back again. 'No?'

'No.' She stood her ground. 'And I very much doubt that you're capable of making me leave, either.'

His face was once again unhealthily pale as his mouth tightened to an angry grim line. 'You don't pull your punches, do you?' he muttered harshly.

Stephanie sighed. 'It isn't my intention to upset you, Mr Simpson—'

'Then get the hell out of my house!' He turned and left the room without a backward glance, his dark hair long and unkempt on his shoulders, and his back stiff with the fury he made no effort to hide.

Leaving Stephanie to sink down wearily into the kitchen chair Jordan had just vacated. She was used to difficult patients—actually relished the challenge of working with them. But dealing with Jordan Simpson was going to be so much harder than Stephanie could ever have imagined a week ago, when she had unknowingly agreed to help Lucan St Claire's brother...

'Changed your mind?' She looked up hopefully an hour later, when she heard the slight unevenness of Jordan's gait as he walked back down the hallway.

'No.' Jordan couldn't say he hadn't been tempted by the delicious smells emanating down the hall from the kitchen and into the study, where he'd sat as this stubborn woman obviously prepared her own dinner. Or that his mouth hadn't watered at the thought of sinking his teeth into a medium-rare steak and a fluffy jacket potato smothered in butter, possibly with a nice light French dressing on the green salad on the side. Tempted, maybe, but there was no way he would give Stephanie McKinley the satisfaction of joining her. 'I thought I told you to leave?' The pristine tidiness of the kitchen showed that she had finished cleaning before even attempting to cook her meal.

She remained comfortably seated at the kitchen table, where she had obviously just finished eating her meal—washed down by a glass of decent-looking red wine if the label on the open bottle on the table was anything to go by. 'Your brother wants me to stay.'

Jordan clenched his jaw. 'You've spoken to him?'

'Not since last week, no.'

'Well, it may have escaped your notice, but Lucan isn't here right now.'

'I have no doubt that he could be here in a matter of hours if I should decide to call him,' Stephanie McKinley came back unconcernedly.

Knowing his arrogant brother as he did, Jordan had no doubt, either, that Lucan was quite capable of climbing into his private helicopter and flying up here if he felt there was a need for him to do so. If Lucan thought that Jordan was being difficult. Which he undoubtedly was!

Jordan limped over to get a glass out of one of the cupboards, poured himself a glass of red wine from the open bottle and then took a sip before answering this increasingly annoying woman. 'If that was a threat then I'm not impressed.'

'It wasn't, and you weren't meant to be.' She grimaced. 'And should you be drinking wine if you're taking medication for pain?'

'This *is* my medication for the pain!' One thing Mulberry Hall did have was a decent wine cellar, and Jordan had helped himself liberally to its contents this past month. A cripple and a drunk; how the mighty had fallen! he thought derisively.

Stephanie McKinley eyed him frowningly. 'Alcohol causes depression—'

'I'm not depressed, damn it!' The glass landed heavily on the table-top as he slammed it down, spilling some of its contents over his hand and onto the wooden surface.

'Okay. But you're angry. Frustrated. And rude.'

'How do you know that I wasn't angry, frustrated and rude before the accident?' Jordan asked.

'You weren't,' Stephanie said quietly as she looked up at him. 'The press would certainly have made something of it if the famous Jordan Simpson were known to be any one of those things.'

Instead of which the media had always written glowing reports of the handsome and charming actor as he escorted leggy blondes to film premieres, or out to dinner at one exclusive LA restaurant or another. Usually looking devastatingly handsome in a black tuxedo or casually tailored clothing, his dark hair still overlong but expertly styled to make the most of his hard and chiselled cheeks and jawline, and the lazily sexy smile that curved those sculptured lips. Not to mention, of course, those mesmerising amber-gold eyes!

A complete contrast to *this* savagely acerbic man, in the crumpled T-shirt and denims he wore this evening, with that growth of beard on his chin and his too-long untidy hair.

'When did you last go to a barber or have a shave?' Stephanie asked.

Jordan picked up the glass and took another long swallow of red wine. 'None of your damned business,' he growled.

'Taking a pride in your appearance—'

'Isn't going to make a damned bit of difference to the fact that my leg is shot to hell.'

'We need to find out why that is,' she pressed.

'No, Stephanie, *you* need to find out why that is if you want to keep what I have no doubt is a very well paying job,' Jordan pointed out. 'But, as I have no intention of letting you anywhere near me or my leg, that's going to prove rather difficult, don't you think?'

Impossible, actually, Stephanie admitted with frustration. Being able to actually assess a patient's disability was more than half the battle. It also affected any and all treatment. Treatment this man had assured her he definitely wasn't going to allow her to give him. She stood up to collect her dirty plates, and carried them over to begin loading them into the dishwasher. 'Would you like me to cook your steak for you now?'

'Tell me, Steph, which part of *get the hell out of my home* didn't you understand earlier?' Jordan St Claire snarled cruelly.

Stephanie drew in a controlling breath. 'As I am neither stupid nor deaf, I understood all of it. I also prefer my…my clients to call me Stephanie or Miss McKinley,' she added primly. Only her family and very close friends were allowed to shorten her name in that way. Besides which, the formality of her full name sounded more professional. And she freely admitted she was having more trouble than usual in keeping her relationship with Jordan Simpson on a professional basis.

Considering the threatened scandal of what Joey called the 'Newman situation', Stephanie definitely needed to keep her relationship with this man—with *all* her patients—on a completely professional basis. If Rosalind Newman's accusations concerning her husband and Stephanie had been true, she knew she would deserve the other woman's vitriol. As it was, she had actually found Richard Newman one of her *least* likeable patients.

Unlike Jordan Simpson, despite his disgraceful temper…

Jordan eyed her mockingly as he refilled his wine glass. 'Why won't you just accept that you're wasting your time with me, *Stephanie*? That I don't want or need you here?'

She raised an eyebrow. 'I agree with the first part of that second statement, at least!'

Jordan's jaw tightened as he saw the challenge in the slight lift of her pointed chin and sparkling green eyes. As he acknowledged once again that his mouth and brain were pushing this woman away at the same time as his body wanted to pull her into his arms and kiss her senseless. He hadn't so much as felt a flicker of physical interest in a woman these past six months, and had wondered in some of his darker moments if perhaps the accident had robbed him of that ability too. The stirring of his thighs just looking at this woman had at least reassured him that wasn't the case, he thought ruefully.

Jordan wondered just what the determinedly professional Stephanie McKinley would do about it if he were to follow through on his instinct to kiss the hell out of her? Run screaming bloody murder into the night, probably, and never darken his door again!

Which, thinking about it, was precisely what Jordan wanted her to do...

He carefully placed his cane against the kitchen table before turning to walk—damn it, hobble!—the short distance that separated them, so that he stood only inches away from the suddenly wary Stephanie McKinley as she pressed herself back against the kitchen cabinet to look up at him with wide apprehensive eyes. 'Not so confident now, hmm, Stephanie?' Jordan deliberately moved closer still.

Stephanie inwardly panicked. She could actually feel the heat of Jordan's body as he stood mere centimetres away from her. She instantly responded to that heat, her breasts seeming to swell, and the nipples becoming hard and full against the thin material of her T-shirt, to her dismay.

Shaved or not, untidy overlong hair notwithstanding, he was undoubtedly every inch the sexually mesmerising A-list actor at that moment!

Stephanie moistened dry lips with the tip of her tongue, at once realising her mistake as she saw the way that seductive golden gaze followed the movement. 'This isn't funny, Jordan—'

'It isn't meant to be.' He moved the small distance that separated them. The aroused hardness of his thighs pressed against Stephanie's own, causing that heat to flare into an uncontrollable flame. 'Is this natural?' Jordan lifted a hand to touch the deep red hair at her temple.

Stephanie frowned. 'You don't seriously think any woman would deliberately dye her hair this colour?' she scorned, in an effort to dispel her discomfort at his close proximity. At having Jordan Simpson touch her in this way.

'It's beautiful,' he murmured appreciatively as he caressed several silky tendrils against his fingertips. 'Unusual.'

Stephanie knew exactly what Jordan was doing. She'd already realised that he was deliberately playing with her as another tactic in getting her to leave. But knowing that didn't make the slightest difference to the way she was responding to his closeness and the light caress of his fingertips as he touched her hair. She could barely breathe—didn't dare breathe—when her aroused breasts were already brushing against the hardness of Jordan's chest and making her ache for even closer contact! 'It's just plain old red.'

'No,' he murmured huskily. 'I've never seen hair quite this colour before. It's auburn and cinnamon, with highlights of red and gold.'

The colour of Stephanie's hair had been the bane of her childhood, and certainly wasn't the feature to mention if he was serious about this seduction. Which he obviously wasn't! 'It's red,' she insisted flatly.

That golden gaze moved slowly over the fullness of

her breasts, lingering appreciatively on those hardened nipples before travelling over the flatness of her stomach and down to her thighs, to linger there speculatively. 'Are you the same—?'

'Don't even go there!' Stephanie interjected sharply, the heat having burned up her cheeks now. 'Just step away from me, Jordan,' she warned.

That golden gaze taunted her. 'Or…?'

She met his gaze challengingly. 'Or I'm afraid I'll have to make you.' Stephanie had taken Ju-Jitsu lessons in self-defence several years ago. She had no doubt she could make him stop, but she wouldn't enjoy doing it to this particular man.

Unnerving Stephanie McKinley, making her too uncomfortable to want to stay on here, had started out as a game to Jordan. It didn't feel like a game any longer, as he saw her physical response to his deliberate seduction. As his erection literally throbbed, so full and hard that it actually hurt as he imagined stripping those figure-hugging jeans from her shapely bottom and thighs, sliding her panties down her long legs before releasing himself, pushing her back against one of the kitchen cabinets and sinking his fullness into her hot and welcoming warmth!

Jordan wanted to do those things so badly—wanted to hear Stephanie McKinley screaming in ecstasy rather than bloody murder—and he could feel the sweat dampening his forehead as he fought against giving in to that impulse.

This physical response to her—the second in an hour or so—had to be because Jordan had been too long without a woman in his bed. With that long red hair, impishly attractive face, and slender if curvaceous body, she wasn't in the *least* his type, damn it!

Jordan's gaze was deliberately mocking as he looked down into her overheated face. 'You just might have been amusing to have around, after all, Stephanie.'

She arched dark brows. 'Might have been?'

'Hmm.' He deliberately moved away from her to limp across the room and pick up his cane. 'Despite your pert little breasts and curvaceous bottom, I still want you out of here,' he bit out contemptuously.

Stephanie eyed him in frustration. Although she had to admit she was relieved Jordan was no longer standing quite so close to her. Or touching her. Or making her completely aware of the thick hardness of his arousal. A physical response that had been undoubtedly because of her!

She ran the dampness of her palms down denim-clad thighs. 'I'm still willing to cook you that steak if you're hungry?' she said huskily.

'That would just be feeding the wrong appetite, Stephanie,' he jibed back.

'Your brother is paying me to take care of your leg, not to go to bed with you!' she exclaimed.

He shrugged. 'That's a pity, when I've decided that right now I need a woman in my bed more than I need a physiotherapist.' Jordan knew he had never needed physical release more than he did at that moment!

'Don't you have a girlfriend you could call?' Stephanie asked curiously.

His face hardened. 'Not any more, no.'

Stephanie looked at him searchingly. Because his parents had divorced when he was a child, Jordan Simpson had never made any secret of his own aversion to the married state. But that hadn't prevented him from having a constant stream of women in his life. Beautiful women. Sophisticated women. Women as unlike Stephanie as it was possible for them to be. Which was the reason she knew that his interest in her wasn't genuine.

'Why not? There must be plenty you could call who would come running.'

He gave a humourless smile. 'Look at me, Stephanie,' he demanded. '*Really* look at me,' he pressed.

Stephanie had already looked. Several times! And, yes, he was obviously thinner, gaunter, grimmer than he had been six months ago, but as far as she was concerned none of that detracted from the fact that he was a compellingly handsome man.

'What am I looking for?'

Jordan gave an impatient snort. 'What was it you called me earlier? A cripple, wasn't it?'

She gasped at the bitterness in his tone. 'No, what I actually said was that *you* obviously believe yourself to be a cripple,' she corrected firmly.

'Maybe because that's what I am?' he said harshly. 'I certainly don't want any woman to be with me just because she feels sorry for me.'

'That's ridiculous—'

'This from the woman who just refused me?' he taunted.

Stephanie rolled her eyes. 'We both know you weren't being serious.'

'Do we?'

'Yes,' she snapped. 'You were just trying to make me leave.'

'Is it working?'

'No,' she told him firmly, determined to ignore the traitorous responses of her own body to this conversation; her breasts felt full and aching, and there was a burning warmth between her thighs…

Knowing that this man was deliberately playing with her in an effort to make her leave made absolutely no difference to the way Stephanie's body responded to him. 'How do you think Lucan will react if I have to call him and tell him I had to leave because you were sexually harassing me?' She looked at him challengingly.

Jordan gave a feral grin. 'He would probably be relieved to know that something has aroused my interest at last.'

Remembering how deeply concerned Lucan St Claire had been about Jordan the previous week, Stephanie thought that might be the case, too!

'*Aroused* being the operative word,' Jordan jeered, and had the pleasure of seeing the blush that re-entered those creamy cheeks.

Stephanie McKinley was really quite beautiful, he realised with a frown, her face impishly lovely, her body feminine and shapely. And his fingers actually itched to release that red-cinnamon-gold hair from its confining braid. He could imagine all that hair splayed out across her luscious nakedness as he feasted hungrily on the fullness of her breasts, before going lower…

He wasn't going to get any sleep tonight, either, if he continued to allow his imagination free rein. In fact a cold shower sounded as if it might be a good idea! 'I'll wish you goodnight, Stephanie.' He gave her another lazy grin before he turned and left the kitchen.

Heading straight for that cold shower.

CHAPTER THREE

'WHERE have you been?' Jordan demanded the following morning, as Stephanie unlocked the kitchen door and let herself back into the house accompanied by a gust of chilling wind, the plastic shopping bags she carried in her hands necessitating she gently nudge the door closed behind her with her foot.

The cold shower Jordan had taken the night before had briefly succeeded in dampening some of his arousal. Unfortunately that arousal had returned with a vengeance the moment he had heard Stephanie making her way up the stairs to use one of the bedrooms for the night.

Because Jordan could no longer negotiate the stairs, Lucan had had the dining room converted into a bedroom before Jordan had moved in, and he'd lain on the bed, staring up at the ceiling, aware of nothing but the throb of his own arousal and easily able to imagine Stephanie McKinley stripping off in the room above his. Jordan had got up to impatiently pull on his clothes before going back out to the kitchen. In the circumstances, the nearly full bottle of red wine on the table had seemed very appealing!

Which had turned out not to be such a good idea on an empty stomach. Consequently, Jordan was like a bear with a sore head this morning, his temples aching almost as much as another part of his anatomy had continued to do for most of the night.

He had already made a pot of strong coffee and brought it to the kitchen table, and had drunk half a cup of the rich and flavoursome brew before he'd become aware of the silence in the rest of the house. Unable to go up the stairs himself, to check on whether Stephanie had left or not, he had instead looked out of the kitchen window to see that her car had gone from the driveway. Leading Jordan to believe that she had taken his advice and left, after all.

Which, strangely, hadn't given him as much satisfaction as he had thought it would. Making him wonder if Lucan could be right when he said Jordan had been here on his own for too long. And now, if he actually felt pleased at the return of the physiotherapist his interfering big brother had hired without even consulting him, he knew he probably had!

'Where does it look like I've been?' Stephanie said sarcastically—a question that required no answer as she dumped the heavy bags of shopping on top of the wooden table before removing her jacket to reveal she wore a yellow fitted T-shirt today, with those low-slung faded blue jeans.

Another short T-shirt, that once again revealed a tantalising glimpse of her flat abdomen and clung to what Jordan was pretty sure were completely bare breasts above…

'Why don't you pour me some of that delicious-smelling coffee while I find the croissants I bought for our breakfast?' she suggested lightly, and she began to look through the bags, that thick braid of red-cinnamon-gold hair falling forward over her shoulder as she did so.

'Yes, ma'am,' he murmured dryly, and he leant back in the wooden chair to snag a clean mug from the side before sitting forward to lift the coffee pot and pour the hot and aromatic brew into both mugs.

'It was a request, not an order,' she sighed.

Jordan raised dark brows as he placed her mug down on the other side of the table, frowning his irritation as he realised he was actually enjoying having his verbal sparring partner back in the house. 'I telephoned Lucan last night,' he informed her coolly.

She continued to search through the bags for the croissants. 'I know.'

Jordan became very still as his gaze narrowed on her suspiciously. 'You *know*?'

'Yep.' Stephanie smiled her satisfaction as she found the box of freshly baked pastries and took it out of the bag, putting it on the table along with the butter and honey she had obviously bought to go with them. 'I telephoned and spoke to him before I went out shopping. He didn't seem too happy about the fact that you woke him up at two o'clock this morning to tell him how much you didn't appreciate him sending me here.'

She lifted the rest of the bags unconcernedly down onto the floor to be unpacked later, moving to take out the plates and knives they needed to eat the croissants before sitting down at the table in the chair opposite his.

Jordan's already frayed temper hadn't been improved the night before by his consumption of two-thirds of a bottle of red wine, and he hadn't even noticed what time it was when the idea to telephone Lucan and take his temper out on his brother had occurred to him. Lucan's growled responses to Jordan's complaints had left him in little doubt as to his big brother's displeasure at the call.

'Then maybe he should have thought of that before he sent you here without asking me!' he snarled.

Stephanie gave a dismissive shrug as she helped herself to one of the deliciously buttery croissants. 'He obviously completely underestimated just how rude and unreasonable you've become.'

Jordan's mouth twisted derisively. 'No doubt you took great pleasure in enlightening him.'

'I didn't need to after you had called him at such a ridiculous hour to complain.' Stephanie took a bite of the butter- and honey-covered croissant, almost groaning at the sensory pleasure she experienced. After being assailed with the delicious aroma of the croissants, first in the supermarket and then on the drive back to the gatehouse; they tasted just as wonderful as she had imagined they would. 'Try one of the croissants, Jordan,' she advised him. 'They might help to get rid of your hangover,' she added naughtily, before taking another delicious bite.

It had been obvious from the used wine glass and the completely empty bottle of red wine she had found left on the table this morning that Jordan must have returned to the kitchen some time during the night. From the look of the dark shadows under his eyes and the pallor in his cheeks the red wine had done little to dispel whatever pain had been keeping him awake.

Although he had at least brushed his hair and shaved this morning, his cleanly shaven jaw revealing its perfect squareness and the beguiling cleft in the centre. A beguilement that Stephanie resisted responding to by concentrating on the fact that he was also wearing a clean white T-shirt and faded jeans, hopefully meaning he wasn't completely bereft of the social niceties, after all. Although she wouldn't like to bet on it!

Stephanie hadn't slept that well herself the night before, aware as she had been of Jordan's presence somewhere in the house, and discovering this morning that there was nothing she could eat for her breakfast—not even bread for toast!—hadn't improved her mood.

A quick telephone call to Lucan St Claire, to confirm that she had arrived safely and so far hadn't been bodily thrown out into the Gloucestershire countryside, had resulted in his informing her that Jordan had already telephoned him during the night with the same news. Although in Jordan's case it had obviously been in the nature of a complaint. A complaint that the older St Claire brother didn't appear in the least concerned about. In fact, his comment had been the one Jordan had predicted—that any response from Jordan was better than the uninterest he normally showed to everything and everyone nowadays.

Stephanie waited until Jordan had taken one of the croissants onto his plate, smothered it in butter and taken a bite before speaking again. 'I decided to refrain from telling your brother that you had decided on sexual innuendo as the best way of getting rid of me.'

Jordan continued to slowly chew the first mouthful of food he'd had for a couple of days, swallowing the buttery pastry before answering her. 'Only because you knew Lucan wouldn't be interested.'

She shrugged. 'Or maybe I'm just saving that complaint for another day.'

Jordan decided there was a lot more to Stephanie McKinley than that unusually coloured hair and a taut and supple body. It surprised him how curious he was to know exactly what that lot more was.

He leant back in his chair. 'I should have asked last night whether or not there's a Mr McKinley waiting for you at home.'

She glanced down at her bare left hand. 'No ring.'

'Not all the married women I know wear a wedding ring,' Jordan drawled.

'That's probably because the married women *you* meet don't want you to know that they're married,' Stephanie pointed out.

Jordan's eyes narrowed. 'I don't get involved with married women.'

'No?'

His mouth firmed. 'No.'

'Because of your parents' divorce?'

Jordan drew in a sharp breath. 'And what do *you* know about my parents' divorce?'

She shrugged as she stood up to place her empty plate neatly inside the dishwasher. 'Only that during interviews you use it as an excuse for never having considered marriage yourself.'

'It happens to be a fact, not an excuse.' He pushed his empty plate away to stand up abruptly.

Stephanie knew she had annoyed Jordan intensely with her mention of his parents' divorce. Not quite the reaction she'd wanted from him, but it was probably better than no reaction at all!

She gave a knowing smile. 'I can't imagine any woman ever daring to be unfaithful to the famous Jordan Simpson.'

His eyes glittered a bright, intense gold. 'My father was unfaithful, not my mother.'

Reason enough, Stephanie decided, for Jordan

never to know that she was being named—albeit completely falsely—as the 'other woman' in an ex-patient's divorce!

He thrust a hand through his hair. 'I'll be in my study for the rest of the morning.'

'Doing what?' She moved so that she was standing in front of the door that led out into the hallway.

He frowned at her. 'None of your damned business!'

'Maybe I could help?'

'And maybe you could stay the hell out of my face!' He glared down at her.

Maybe getting in his face hadn't been such a good idea, Stephanie recognised uncomfortably, as she became aware of the heat of Jordan's body and the glittering intensity of those mesmerising gold-coloured eyes. 'When I spoke to Lucan this morning, he mentioned that there's a heated indoor pool at Mulberry Hall…'

Jordan raised a brow. 'And?'

'And a swim might be fun.'

Those gold eyes hardened. 'Am I right in thinking it might also be regarded as good exercise to strengthen the muscles in my leg?'

Stephanie felt the guilty heat of colour in her cheeks and her expression became defensive. 'What's wrong with that?'

He shrugged those wide and powerful shoulders. 'Absolutely nothing.' His mouth thinned. '*If* I wanted to exercise the muscles in my leg. Which I *don't*,' he added emphatically.

She sighed. 'Why don't you?'

A nerve pulsed in his tightly clenched jaw. 'Get out of my way, Stephanie.'

She gave a firm shake of her head, her chin raised.

She refused to move. 'Not until you explain to me why you don't even seem to want to *try* to get back the full mobility of your leg.'

A red haze seemed to pass in front of Jordan's eyes as this woman's persistent questions managed to pierce his armour once again. 'Don't be so stupid!'

'So you *do* want to get back the use of your leg?'

'What I want and what I've got are two different things,' he said pointedly.

Stephanie put a hand on his arm. 'Then prove me wrong and come swimming with me this morning.'

'Now who's playing games?'

'Come on, Jordan, it will be fun,' she cajoled.

'Don't force me into making you move, Stephanie,' he bit out between gritted teeth.

'Could you do that?' Her chin rose another determined notch. 'Do you really think you're physically capable at the moment of making me—or anyone else—do anything?'

Jordan's fingers tightened about his cane as the taunt struck him with the force of a blow. 'You vicious little—!'

She gave an unconcerned shrug. 'No one said you had to like me in order for me to help you.'

'I don't remember asking for your help,' he ground out as his eyes glittered down at her in warning.

'Whether you ask for it or not, you certainly need it.'

Jordan breathed deeply as he continued to glare down at Stephanie McKinley's five feet six inches of slender shapeliness. And stubbornness. Let's not forget the bone-deep stubbornness so evident in her determined expression, Jordan told himself.

He deliberately, slowly, allowed his gaze to move lower, to where her breasts pressed against her T-shirt.

Having him staring so intently at her breasts wasn't exactly conducive to her feeling as if she were in control of this situation, Stephanie acknowledged. And she had decided during her own virtually sleepless night that being in control was going to be necessary from now on, if she was going to get anywhere in bringing about this man's recuperation.

Especially as that gaze alone was enough to cause her nipples to harden noticeably beneath the soft material of her T-shirt, so that they now stood out like ripe berries begging to be eaten!

Stephanie could never remember feeling this sexual tension with any of the men she had dated. Or the flare of electricity that seemed to spark between herself and Jordan whenever they were in a room together. Or the need to halt the impulse she felt to wrap her arms protectively over those betraying breasts!

She determinedly continued to resist that impulse as she kept her gaze fixed steadily on Jordan's arrogantly handsome face. Instead, she drew in an irritated breath. 'I'm here on a professional basis, Mr Simpson—or Mr St Claire—whatever I'm to call you—not to provide you with amusement!'

Jordan wasn't as sure of that as Stephanie appeared to be. For days, weeks after the accident, there had been dozens of visitors to the hospital where he had been taken for treatment—many of them women he had been involved with in the past or who would have liked to have become involved with him in the future. Not a single one of them had succeeded in arousing the heated response in him that Stephanie McKinley had almost from the moment he'd first looked at her. Nor given him the perverse enjoyment he felt during their verbal exchanges…

Admittedly, he had been in even more pain immediately after the accident than he was now, and so hardly in the mood for physical arousal. But he was still in a lot of pain, and he only had to look at Stephanie to know he wanted to strip her bare and lie her down on the nearest bed, before kissing and caressing every freckled inch of her.

He focused his gaze on the fullness of her provocatively pouting mouth. Lips that Jordan could all too easily imagine taking him to the heights of pleasure…

'Parts of your body don't seem to be in agreement with that statement,' he taunted, with a knowing glance at her full and obviously aroused breasts.

Stephanie's cheeks burned uncomfortably as she felt an increase in the sexual tension that had flared so suddenly between the two of them. 'It's cold in here,' she excused lamely.

Jordan chuckled softly. 'Strange…it feels the opposite to me.'

To Stephanie too. The sexual heat between them was enough to make her cheeks flush even hotter. 'I won't delay you any longer,' she muttered as she finally stepped aside to allow Jordan to leave. Willing him to leave so that she could try to calm her overheated body.

Jordan leant on his cane and walked slowly over to the door. 'Let me know if you decide to leave, after all.'

'Why, do you intend to come and wave me off?' she shot back dryly.

'No, I'd just like to have the key to the door returned before you leave,' came his parting shot, and he gave her one last challenging glance before leaving the kitchen.

Stephanie sank back down into the kitchen chair once she was alone, and poured herself another cup of the deliciously strong but now cooling coffee Jordan had made earlier.

What *was* it about the male patients she had worked with recently? She was pretty sure she hadn't suddenly turned into some sort of sex siren or temptress, so it had to be that her job brought her into such close proximity to those patients that it made her an easy target.

Whatever the reason, Stephanie knew she was going to have much more trouble resisting Jordan's advances than she ever had the lecherous and totally obnoxious Richard Newman's!

CHAPTER FOUR

'WHAT do you want now?' Jordan asked impatiently as he looked across the desk to where Stephanie loitered in the open doorway of the study where he had been working for the last hour.

She was completely undeterred by his obvious lack of enthusiasm. 'I was thinking of going for a walk, and wondered if you would care to join me?'

Jordan's eyes narrowed as he sat back in the leather chair behind the desk. 'I'm not sure if you're being deliberately insensitive again, or just a pain.'

'Neither.' Stephanie smiled.

She had tidied and cleaned the kitchen after breakfast, dusted and vacuumed the sitting room—which didn't look as if anyone had sat in there for some time—and made some fresh chicken soup for lunch and left it simmering on top of the Aga. On the basis that seeing that Jordan had a healthy and varied diet was part of her job of restoring him back to full health.

With nothing else left to do, Stephanie was becoming a little bored with her own company. 'We don't have to go far, Jordan,' she added cajolingly. 'You could just take me up to Mulberry Hall and show me around if you don't feel like going any further than that.'

Jordan eyed her suspiciously. 'Does this I'm-a-little-girl-in-need-of-company routine usually work?'

'I'm not in need of company, and it isn't a routine,' she denied. 'I just thought some fresh air might be nice.'

'And exercise,' he drawled derisively. 'Let's not forget the exercise!'

'God, you're a grump.' Stephanie sighed with frustration as she turned away.

'Hey, I don't remember saying I wouldn't go with you.'

Stephanie turned back slowly. 'Does that mean you will?'

'Why not?' Jordan said, and he picked up his cane and stood up. He doubted he would be able to get any more work done on the film script this morning now anyway, knowing that Stephanie was wandering about the estate. 'Although showing you round Mulberry Hall might prove a little difficult when I can't get up stairs,' he added with a scowl.

'You can always wait downstairs while I go and take a look upstairs,' she reasoned practically.

'You might have a sudden urge to try one of the four-poster beds!' Jordan teased.

'Oh, give it a break, Jordan,' the little redhead growled.

He shrugged. 'I can't see any point in you staying on here if I can't make life uncomfortable for you.'

Neither could Stephanie at the moment, but she lived in hope that she might eventually be able to change Jordan's mind about accepting her professional help. In the meantime, getting him to take a walk with her was better than nothing.

'I'll just go upstairs and get my thicker jacket. It's quite cold outside for October.'

'If that was your subtle way of telling me that I need to wrap up warm too, then I strongly advise you not to treat me like a child,' Jordan told her.

'I wasn't treating you like a—' She stopped, frowning as she realised that was exactly what she had been doing. In an effort, perhaps, to try and keep their relationship on a professional footing rather than the flirtatious one Jordan kept reducing it to with his questionable remarks. 'I—' She broke off again as the telephone began to ring.

Well…one of them. There was an extension for the landline on the desktop, as well as two mobiles—one black and one silver. Stephanie could understand the landline, but who needed two mobiles, for goodness' sake?

Jordan picked up the black mobile, checking the caller ID before taking the call. 'Hi, Crista,' he said, and he turned his back on Stephanie to look out of the window.

Stephanie stared at the broad expanse of that muscled back, at the way the white T-shirt stretched tautly over his shoulders, and debated whether she should go or stay. The call was obviously private. From Crista Moore, the woman Jordan had been reportedly involved with before his accident.

'Stay!' Jordan barked as he turned and saw that Stephanie was about to leave.

'Woof, woof!' She wrinkled her nose at him before going ahead and leaving anyway.

Jordan found himself smiling as he watched the sway of those curvaceous hips and taut bottom as Stephanie walked down the hallway. She really was the most—

'No, I wasn't talking to you, Crista,' he said lightly into the receiver as the caller queried his last comment. 'Oh, just a—an associate of my brother's,' he said evasively, easily able to imagine the tall, slender blonde actress as she sat in her apartment in LA.

Of all the people Jordan had known before the accident, Crista was definitely the most persistent—calling him at least once a week to see how he was and when he would be coming back to LA. As Jordan had no intention of ever resuming their relationship, any more than he had immediate plans to return to LA, he usually kept those telephone calls short.

Even so, Stephanie was sitting at the kitchen table impatiently waiting for him by the time Jordan had ended the call and collected his coat. 'Hmm, something smells good.' He sniffed appreciatively at the saucepan he could see simmering on top of the Aga.

'Soup for lunch,' she supplied economically as she stood up to pull on a heavy black jacket. 'No, I *don't* see that as acting the housekeeper,' she defended irritably as Jordan raised mocking brows. 'For your body to be healthy you need to eat healthily, that's all.'

He smiled. 'So you're saying you only made lunch because you consider feeding me a part of my treatment?'

Those green eyes narrowed. 'Exactly.'

'If you say so.'

'Jordan—'

'Stephanie?'

She wasn't fooled for a moment by Jordan's too-innocent expression, knowing he was just trying to irritate her again. And obviously succeeding! 'Why do you need two mobile phones?' she asked, as she pulled on a pair of black gloves to keep her hands warm.

A slight frown appeared between those amber-gold eyes. 'What?'

She shrugged. 'I noticed earlier that there were two mobiles on the desk in the study, and I was just curious as to why you would need two when most people manage fine with just one?'

'Maybe because I'm two people?' Jordan finally replied, deciding that Stephanie McKinley was far too observant for his comfort sometimes.

She arched auburn brows. 'Because you're both Jordan Simpson and Jordan St Claire?'

'Yes.'

'Why did you change your name when you became an actor? Jordan St Claire is quite a charismatic name—'

'Are we going for this walk or not?' Jordan's mouth thinned as he stepped forward and pointedly opened the back door for her.

'We are.' Stephanie nodded as she stepped outside. 'So you actually consider Jordan Simpson and Jordan St Claire to be two distinctly different people?' she persisted as he locked the door behind them before joining her on the path.

Jordan didn't *consider* them to be anything—they *were* two distinctly different people! As different as night and day. And non-interchangeable. 'Could we just get this walk over with, do you think?' he barked, before striding off in the direction of Mulberry Hall.

'Of course.' Stephanie deliberately measured her strides so that they were in step with his much slower ones. 'You never considered working in the St Claire Corporation?' she prompted curiously.

It was a curiosity that was probably understandable in the circumstances. Except Jordan wasn't presently known for his understanding! 'Have you ever heard of maintaining a companionable silence when out walking?'

Of course Stephanie had heard of it; it just wasn't something that was ever likely to happen between herself and Jordan! An awkward silence, perhaps. An uncomfortable silence, even. A totally physically aware one, certainly. At least on her part… The scowl on Jordan's arrogantly handsome face as he stomped along beside her didn't give the impression that he was in the least aware of her, or anyone else for that matter.

'Wow!'

Jordan leant tiredly against one of the four marble pillars in the magnificent hallway of Mulberry Hall as Stephanie gazed up in awe at the huge Venetian glass chandelier hanging down from the frescoed ceiling high above them. Jordan's leg was aching too much from the half-mile or so walk over here for him to share her enthusiasm. Besides, he had seen the inside of Mulberry Hall dozens of times before.

'This is… I mean, *wow*!'

'I get that you're in awe,' Jordan drawled dryly as he watched her wandering around the cavernous hallway, admiring the beautiful marble floor and statuary.

'And you aren't?' Her eyes were wide with accusation.

'Not particularly, no,' Jordan muttered as he pushed himself away from the pillar to lean heavily on his cane and walk towards the main salon at the front of the house.

Stephanie trailed slowly along behind him, her eyes bright with pleasure as she came to stand on the threshold of the room, looking at the beautiful gold and cream decor and delicate Regency furniture. 'Has Lucan never thought of opening this up to the public?'

'Definitely not.' Jordan almost laughed at the thought of the expression of disgust that would appear on his eldest brother's face if anyone dared to suggest he should open the doors of Mulberry Hall to all and sundry. 'I don't recommend that you suggest it to him, either—unless you want to feel the icy blast of his complete disapproval.'

'But it seems such a waste.' Stephanie frowned. 'The building itself must be very old.'

'Early Elizabethan, I believe.'

Stephanie crossed the room to lightly touch the beautiful ornate gold frame about the huge mirror above the white fireplace. 'Did Lucan buy it completely furnished like this?' There were ornaments and lamps on the surfaces of the many side tables, and a large dresser along one wall, as well as a beautiful Ormolu clock on top of the fireplace.

Jordan gave an uninterested shrug. 'As far as I'm aware some of this furniture has been here for a couple of hundred years at least.'

'I wonder what happened to the family that lived here?' Stephanie murmured. 'It must have been someone titled, don't you think?'

Jordan nodded. 'The Dukes of Stourbridge.'

Stephanie sighed. 'It's such a pity that so many of the old titles have either become extinct or fallen into disuse.'

'Yes, a pity,' Jordan drawled dryly.

'Do you suppose Lucan intends to live here once he's married? It was just a thought,' she defended as Jordan gave a shout of laughter. 'You say that he doesn't intend opening it to the public, but he must intend doing something with it, surely?'

'Sorry, I was just trying to imagine Lucan married,' Jordan gasped, his shoulders still shaking slightly. 'No, I just can't see it, I'm afraid.'

Stephanie couldn't imagine the cold and self-contained man she had met the previous week madly in love and married, either. 'I wonder why he bothered to buy it, then?'

'I never try to second-guess Lucan, and I'd advise you not to bother trying, either,' Jordan suggested as he turned away. 'Do you want to see the pool at the back of the house now?' he offered, when he saw Stephanie hadn't moved from in front of the fireplace.

'Philistine,' she accused him good-naturedly as she followed him back out into the incredible marble hallway.

Stephanie had visited several country estates in the past that had been open to the public, but never an empty one that looked quite so much as if someone still lived there. There were paintings on all the walls, ornaments and antique mirrors everywhere, and there was even a silver tray on the stand in the hallway that looked as if it were waiting for visiting cards to be placed upon it. In fact the whole house had the look of expecting the master of the house—the Duke of Stourbridge—to walk through the front doorway at any moment.

'Lucan has a caretaker for the grounds, and his wife keeps the inside of the house free of dust,' Jordan explained when Stephanie said as much to him.

'Even so, it seems a shame that no one actually lives here...' Stephanie looked about her wistfully.

'It's really not the sort of place you could ever call

home, now, is it?' Jordan scorned. 'That you would ever really *want* to call home,' he added.

Stephanie stood at the bottom of the wide and sweeping staircase that led up the gallery above, wondering how many beautiful women had stood poised at the top of that staircase, in gowns from the Elizabethan period to now, to be admired by the men they loved as they floated down those stairs and into their waiting arms. Dozens of them, probably. And now Mulberry Hall stood empty, apart from the caretaker and his wife who obviously lived somewhere else on the estate, when it should have been full of love and the laughter of children.

'I suppose not,' she agreed slowly, before following him.

Jordan had nothing more to add to that particular conversation. Had no intention of telling the already over-curious Stephanie McKinley that Lucan hadn't bought Mulberry Hall at all, that he was in fact the current and fifteenth Duke of Stourbridge. Which consequently made *him* Lord Jordan St Claire and his twin brother Lord Gideon St Claire—a little known fact that his using the professional name of Simpson had helped keep from the public in general.

The three brothers had spent their early childhood growing up at Mulberry Hall. Until their Scottish mother had discovered that their father, the fourteenth Duke of Stourbridge, had been keeping a mistress in the village. After the separation Molly had decided to move back to her native Edinburgh, and had taken her three sons with her.

Obviously the three boys had come back to Mulberry Hall on visits to their father, but they had all much preferred the rambling untidiness of their home in

Edinburgh to the stiff formality of life at Mulberry Hall. Besides which, none of the three brothers had ever really forgiven their father for his unfaithfulness to their gentle and beautiful mother.

As a consequence, when the three boys had reached an age where they could choose to visit or not, they had all chosen not to come anywhere near Mulberry Hall or their father again. That aversion to the place hadn't changed in the least when their father had died eight years ago and Lucan had inherited the title.

They had all had their own lives by then. Lucan in the cut-throat world of business, Jordan in acting and Gideon in law. None of them had needed or wanted the restrictions of life at Mulberry Hall. Although it had so far proved an invaluable bolt-hole for Jordan after he had felt the need to leave the States in an effort to elude the press that still hounded his every move months after the accident…

'You wouldn't even realise this was here from the front of the house.' Stephanie stood at the edge of the full-length pool to look admiringly at the surrounding statuary and greenery that made up the low and heated pool room built onto the back of Mulberry Hall.

'I think that was the idea.' Jordan made no effort to hide his sarcasm.

She shot him an impatient glance as she slipped off her jacket in the heat of the room. 'It's really warm in here, and the water looks very inviting; are you sure you won't change your mind about going for a swim?'

He quirked a wicked brow at her. 'I might consider it if you intend skinny-dipping.'

'Stop changing the subject, Jordan.' Stephanie rounded on him. 'You have the ideal facility here for gently exercising your leg, and yet you refuse to use it.'

'Because I don't want to exercise my leg—gently or otherwise,' Jordan stated firmly.

'Why not?'

'And you accuse *me* of being stubborn!' His eyes glittered deeply gold.

'That's because you are!'

'And you really think that your constant nagging on the subject is going to make me change my mind?' Jordan said.

Stephanie gasped. 'I do not nag!'

'Yes. You. Do.' The two of them were now standing almost nose to nose as Jordan glared down at Stephanie and she raised her chin in challenge. 'Oh, to hell with this!' He threw his cane down onto one of the loungers that surrounded the pool, then pulled Stephanie hard against his body before bending his head and savagely claiming her mouth with his.

The forceful kiss was so unexpected that she didn't even have time to resist its sensual pull as her lips parted beneath Jordan's, her coat slipping from her fingers as she moved her hands up to clasp those wide and muscled shoulders in an effort to keep her balance.

Her back arched instinctively, pushing her breasts against the hard wall of his chest, the proximity instantly making her aware of how swollen her nipples were, how they ached for the touch of those same hands that now moved so restlessly down the slenderness of her spine.

Suddenly she realised exactly how inappropriate allowing Jordan to kiss her actually was. Of how easily her behaviour could be misconstrued if he were ever to learn of Rosalind Newman's outrageous accusations.

It was as if a bucket of icy cold water had been thrown over her. She broke the kiss to move back abruptly, her eyes widening in alarm as she realised that even that slight movement had unbalanced Jordan—and his hands took a tight grip of her arms as he began to fall back towards the pool!

CHAPTER FIVE

'DID you intend that to happen?' Jordan accused as he surfaced and pushed back the wet dark hair that had fallen over his eyes.

His anger was all the stronger for the realisation that he couldn't even do a simple thing like kiss a woman without making a complete fool of himself. Without demonstrating just how incapacitated he was!

Stephanie had been on the verge of laughing at their predicament as she surfaced beside him, but one look at Jordan's grimly annoyed face was enough to kill that laughter dead as she trod water beside him to stay afloat.

Then she recalled exactly what they had been doing before they fell into the water…

Dear God!

How could she have let that happen? *Why* had she let that happen? It made her position here untenable. Almost impossible. She—

'What do you mean, did *I* intend that to happen?' She frowned darkly as Jordan's accusation finally sank into her shocked brain. 'Do you think that I—that we—that I deliberately let you kiss me with the intention of—?'

'Pushing me in?' Jordan finished savagely as he began to swim effortlessly to the side of the pool. 'Yes,

Stephanie, that's exactly what I think,' he said, as he used the strength of his arms to lever himself up and out onto the side of the pool.

Stephanie swam after him. 'You can't seriously believe that, Jordan?'

'Oh, yeah, Stephanie, I can.'

'But—'

'You wanted me in the pool, and that's exactly where I ended up.' Jordan was breathing hard from the exertion, leaving a trail of water behind him as he limped over to the cupboard where the towels were kept, taking one out to rub the excess water from his dripping wet hair. 'If nothing else, I have to give you full marks for professional dedication.' He threw the damp towel down disgustedly onto a lounger. 'In fact I'll be sure to mention to Lucan exactly how dedicated you are when I call him later and tell him I've kicked your shapely little bottom off the estate.'

Stephanie stood on the side of the pool too now, as angry as Jordan. He *really* believed that in the midst of being kissed by him she'd had the presence of mind to deliberately overbalance him as a way of forcing him into the swimming pool? She didn't have that sort of control—in fact much longer in Jordan's arms, being kissed by him, and she would have been completely *out* of control!

'Now, just a minute—'

'I believe I've already wasted enough of my time on you for one day.' Jordan glowered at her from between narrowed lids before his expression turned to a scowl of dark and savage disgust and he looked down to pull the cold dampness of his T-shirt away from his chest.

Stephanie couldn't take her gaze away from the muscled perfection of that chest, which was clearly visible through the wet T-shirt. She could feel her face burning with the memory of how much she had wanted to touch that muscled chest a few minutes ago. Of how much she had wanted to touch and caress all of him.

She turned away to take a towel from the cupboard and dry herself off as a way of hiding the burning in her cheeks, her mind racing with the enormity of what had just happened. World-famous actor Jordan Simpson had just kissed *her*, Stephanie McKinley.

Before accusing her of deliberately encouraging him so that she could push him into the pool! She certainly *hadn't* done it deliberately, but had she encouraged him to kiss her? Stephanie didn't think that she had…although she doubted that Rosalind Newman, for one, would believe that! This was terrible. She was fed up with being portrayed as some kind of scarlet woman. This would surely be the complete end of Stephanie's professional career if Jordan went ahead and voiced his accusations about her to the cold and arrogant Lucan St Claire.

Stephanie felt ill. Nauseous. Could literally feel the heat leaving her cheeks. She stumbled over to one of the loungers to collapse onto it as her knees gave way beneath her.

She might be able to fight one accusation of indulging in sexual indiscretion with a patient—but no one was going to believe two such accusations. Even if Stephanie managed to prove her innocence, some of the mud was sure to stick. Her professional reputation would be in tatters—

'What's wrong, Stephanie?' Jordan had moved so that he now towered over her.

She blinked back the tears that were threatening to fall before looking up at him. God, they both looked such a mess: hair wet and tangled, their clothes clinging to them damply. Although maybe she should feel grateful they were still wearing any clothes at all after the way she had responded to Jordan's kiss!

She shook her head as she murmured heavily, 'That should never have happened…'

No, it shouldn't, Jordan accepted, disgusted with himself. He had meant to stay as far away from this woman as possible, and hope that his non-cooperation would eventually persuade her into leaving. Kissing her as if he wanted to eat every delectable part of her could hardly be called non-cooperation on his part!

Although Stephanie's guilt over a kiss was a little over the top, wasn't it?

Jordan frowned as he stared down into green eyes awash with unshed tears. As he remembered how Stephanie's responses had been so sweet, so addictive… So much so that Jordan was still aroused, that hardness clearly visible against the clinging denim material of his jeans.

Obviously the unexpected swim had been no more effective in dampening his desire for this woman than the cold shower had the night before.

Hell!

She blinked back those tears. 'I really didn't deliberately push you into the pool, Jordan.'

Jordan already knew that—just as he knew it was himself he was angry with and not Stephanie. 'I think it's better if we both forget the whole incident, don't you?' he suggested huskily.

'Yes,' she breathed raggedly.

He thrust a hand through his wet hair. 'I suggest we both go back to the gatehouse now, and get out of these wet clothes before taking a shower.'

'Before I leave?'

'I think that would be the best thing for both of us,' he confirmed heavily.

'Just as well I didn't unpack completely last night, isn't it?' Stephanie muttered dully as she stood up, giving Jordan a clear view of how the yellow T-shirt clung to the fullness of her bare breasts, clearly outlining the hard, berry-pink nipples he hadn't quite got around to touching earlier.

He glanced away, but not quickly enough to stop his own arousal from throbbing anew. 'Are you coming back to the house or not?' he bit out, with a return of his impatience.

'I'm coming.' Stephanie picked up her jacket and slowly followed him outside.

She continued to inwardly bombard herself with self-recriminations as they walked back to the gatehouse in complete and uncomfortable silence. No matter how many times she went over the incident in her mind—whether she'd encouraged him or not—Stephanie knew that she shouldn't have allowed that kiss with Jordan to happen. It didn't really matter that she hadn't planned it. Or that it still made her go hot all over just thinking about it!

The heat had completely dissipated by the time they had walked the half-mile or so back to the gatehouse, with the cold wind blowing through her wet clothing, and Stephanie's teeth were literally chattering. Her face felt blue with the cold by the time Jordan unlocked the back door and allowed her to precede him into the warm and delicious-smelling kitchen.

'You need to go upstairs and take a shower and put on some dry clothes,' Jordan said again, as he saw how cold Stephanie was.

'I—yes. Fine.' She turned away to hang her coat on the back of one of the chairs. 'You should do the same.'

'I know what I need to do, Stephanie,' Jordan scowled. 'When you come back we'll sit down and eat the soup you've made.'

She turned, her eyes wide. 'But I thought you wanted me to leave.'

His mouth firmed. 'Not before you've eaten something warm. I would hate for you to get back to London only to be admitted to hospital suffering from pneumonia,' he explained as she frowned.

Stephanie looked at him searchingly before nodding slowly. 'Some hot soup would be nice.'

'Fine,' he said tersely. 'Well?' he added a second later, as she made no effort to leave.

She swallowed hard. 'I—I just want you to know that I really didn't do anything deliberate to make us both fall into the swimming pool,' she told him, one last time before leaving to go up the stairs.

Jordan drew in a deep breath once he was alone, his hands clenched at his sides, his expression bleak, knowing that his accident had obviously robbed him of his sense of humour as well as the mobility in his right leg. At any other time he would have found it funny that the two of them had fallen into the swimming pool.

Stephanie was the first woman he had even attempted to make love to since his accident six months ago. *Attempted* being an accurate description of the fiasco it had turned into!

Stephanie's sensuously lush mouth had been so delicious to kiss. Her body so responsive as it had moulded against his own. Jordan had been totally aroused as he'd kissed her—so aroused, in fact, that he had forgotten everything else. Including the weakness of his right hip and leg…

Jordan knew without a doubt that Stephanie wasn't the one responsible for making the two of them lose their balance and fall into the pool. He was only too aware of why it had happened, and exactly why he had been so angry afterwards. He had unthinkingly put his weight onto his right hip, and it had just collapsed beneath him and toppled them both into the water.

It all went to prove that he couldn't even kiss a woman any more without the embarrassment and utter humiliation of having his leg give way. It was more than a man could stand!

'I've decided I'm not leaving, after all,' Stephanie announced when she returned down the stairs half an hour later. She stood her ground determinedly in the kitchen doorway as Jordan turned to frown at her from where he stood in front of the Aga, stirring the soup.

He had obviously taken advantage of her absence to shower and change into dry jeans and a thin black cashmere sweater. The overlong darkness of his hair looked almost dry too, although there was a grim set to his mouth to add to his icy expression—an expression that Stephanie refused to be cowed by as much as she refused to leave.

She had run herself a bath rather than taking the suggested shower, deciding she needed to immerse herself fully in hot water in order to soak the chill from her bones. She'd had time to think once she had sunk her shoulders beneath the hot and scented bubble bath.

Okay, so she accepted that she shouldn't have let Jordan kiss her. Nor should she have responded to that kiss. She also accepted that those things made continuing to stay on here awkward, to say the least. But awkward in a personal way, not a professional one.

She had no intention of allowing Lucan to actually pay her a wage until Jordan let her work with him professionally. Which meant that technically Jordan wasn't her patient yet. He wouldn't become so until Stephanie actually did something professional for or to him. Her constant arguments with him about his need for treatment really didn't count. Neither did making him a nourishing soup for lunch.

If Stephanie left now then she would be admitting professional defeat. She was guilty of nothing of a personal nature except finding the 'magnetically handsome' Jordan Simpson magnetically handsome! Something that any woman with an ounce of red blood in her veins would have to admit to, surely?

She would be admitting that professionally she was as incapable of getting anywhere with the stubbornly determined actor as all the other physiotherapists who had tried to work with him these last six months. That sort of defeat had never been an option as far as Stephanie was concerned. She wouldn't accept it now with Jordan, either.

She entered the kitchen fully. 'I said—'

'I heard what you said,' Jordan drawled as he considered her through lowered lids. 'I'm just surprised that you still think it's your decision to make.'

'Actually, it's your brother's,' she acknowledged lightly. 'Once I start working for him. Which I'm not doing at the moment,' she added sweetly.

Those gold-coloured eyes glittered icily. 'And you don't believe that attempting to drown his brother is reason enough for Lucan to want to dispense with your services altogether?'

'Attempting to drown—?' Stephanie gave a disbelieving shake of her head, her gaze incredulous. 'Don't you think that's a slight exaggeration?'

'Perhaps. Except you couldn't have known whether or not I could actually swim when you pushed me into the water.' He arched challenging brows.

'I did *not* push you in.'

'Prove it.'

Her cheeks were flushed with temper. 'I can no more prove that than you can prove otherwise!'

Jordan shrugged. 'All of that aside, you must know as well as I do that the two of us staying here together is even less feasible now than it was before.'

'I'm not leaving,' she repeated stubbornly.

Impasse, Jordan acknowledged in sheer frustration. Stephanie was refusing to leave, and this morning had certainly proved that he sure as hell couldn't make her! At least, not physically…

Jordan deliberately crossed the kitchen so that he stood only inches away from her. Close enough to feel the heat of her body in the close-fitting green jumper and blue jeans she had changed into. 'If you stay on here then I guarantee that what happened between us this morning will happen again,' he warned her huskily.

Those green eyes widened in alarm even as her cheeks warmed with colour. Evidence that she wasn't as self-possessed about what had happened earlier as she wished to appear, he thought smugly.

She shook her head. 'Not if I don't want it to.'

'But you *do* want it to, Stephanie.' Jordan held her gaze with his as he curved his hand about one of those over-heated cheeks. He saw with satisfaction the way the blood pulsed at her temples. His gaze moved down and he watched the way she moistened her lips nervously. He glanced even lower and saw the unmistakable signs of her nipples pressing against the soft wool of her sweater. 'Don't you?' he murmured knowingly.

There was a look of panic in her eyes now. 'No, I—'

'Yes, Stephanie,' Jordan insisted gently as he ran the pad of his thumb lightly across the soft pout of her lips and felt the way they quivered beneath his caress. 'Your response to my touch clearly says yes.'

She swallowed hard. 'You're still trying to force me into leaving.'

'Is it working?' Jordan taunted. He knew damn well that it was; he wasn't so out of practice that he didn't know when a woman was responding to him! 'I won't stop at kissing next time, Stephanie,' he warned her. 'Next time I'll kiss and touch you until you're so aching and wet for me that you'll be begging me to make love to you!'

He spoke so forcefully, so graphically, that Stephanie had no trouble whatsoever in imagining them naked in bed together, skin moving on skin, their breathing ragged and their bodies entangled as they caressed and kissed each other to completion.

Just thinking of the possibility of it made Stephanie aroused all over again.

She had made her decision to stay on here when she was upstairs, well away from Jordan's physically disturbing presence. Calmly. Coolly. But they weren't emotions Stephanie could maintain when she was actually in his presence.

She raised her chin stubbornly to meet the mockery of his gaze head-on. 'Just because the tabloids often scream out headlines about the "eligible and sexy Jordan Simpson" as he escorts his latest airhead somewhere, it doesn't mean that every woman you meet is going to fall down adoringly at your feet. Or any other part of your anatomy, for that matter,' she added scathingly.

He gave a hard smile. 'No?'

'No!' Stephanie snapped as she heard the deliberate challenge in his tone.

'Flattered as I am that you've bothered to read those tabloids—'

'I didn't say I had read them, only that I'd seen the headlines,' she defended hotly.

He gave her a knowing look. 'If you say so.'

'I do!'

Jordan shrugged. 'I'm not answerable for what the tabloids choose to print about me, Stephanie. Or to the women I've dated in the past.'

'Don't you mean currently?' Stephanie accused. 'That *was* Crista Moore who telephoned you this morning, wasn't it?'

The name Crista really was too unusual for Jordan's earlier caller to have been anyone else. Which meant he was probably still involved with the beautiful actress…

Which made letting him kiss her even more stupid on Stephanie's part!

'What if it was?' he said.

Her eyes narrowed. 'Maybe you should just stick to one airhead at a time!'

'I wouldn't put you in the airhead category, Stephanie,' he teased.

'*We* aren't dating!'

'We aren't anything yet,' Jordan accepted dryly. 'But if you insist on staying on here we're most definitely going to be something.'

Stephanie's cheeks blushed hotly. 'You can't possibly know that.'

'Would you like me to show you?'

'You arrogant, overbearing, self—'

'Sticks and stones, Stephanie…'

'No, it's the truth,' she maintained forcefully. 'You may have—may have caught me slightly off-guard this morning when you kissed me, but it won't happen again.'

'No?' He moved closer to her.

Stephanie stood her ground. 'No!'

His eyes gleamed with amusement. 'You seem slightly—flustered…'

'I'm getting rather annoyed, actually,' she flared back at him.

Jordan narrowed shrewd eyes. 'Just not annoyed enough to leave?'

'No!'

'Fine.' His mouth firmed as he finally stepped away from her, making her sigh inwardly in relief. 'Have it your own way. Just don't say I didn't warn you.'

It sounded more like a threat to Stephanie than a warning.

A threat of intent.

CHAPTER SIX

'I'M GOING back to my study to work.' Jordan reached for his cane to stand up from the table where they had just sat in total silence eating the warming soup.

It had been an uncomfortable silence. A silence full of awareness. Mental. Emotional. But most of all physical.

Jordan still had no explanation at to why he was even attracted to the determined and difficult physiotherapist. He had never been attracted to green-eyed redheads of medium height and medium build before now. He had certainly never found argumentative women in the least appealing.

Stephanie McKinley was all those things and more.

The 'more' being her mulish stubbornness in refusing to leave Mulberry Hall!

Well, just because *she* wouldn't leave there was no reason for Jordan to have to stay in the same room as her. 'I don't want to be disturbed for the rest of the afternoon, but you can come and get me when dinner's ready,' he said autocratically as Stephanie stood up to clear the table.

'Yes, My Lord.' She turned to give him a mocking curtsy. 'Certainly, My Lord.'

Jordan drew in a sharp breath even as his gaze narrowed on her suspiciously. He had assumed earlier that she knew nothing about the history of the St Claire family. She had certainly given no indication when they'd talked earlier that she had connected Jordan's family with the Dukes of Stourbridge, or that she knew he really was a lord in truth.

There was no indication of that knowledge in Stephanie's mischievous expression now, either—only a glint of mocking laughter in those expressive green eyes to go with that curtsy she had just given him.

Jordan relaxed. 'If I really were a lord, and this were a few hundred years ago, then I would have put you out onto the streets to starve by now for your insolence.'

She gave a rueful shake of her head. 'Then how lucky it is for me that the time of the feudal overlord is long gone.'

Perhaps someone should have mentioned that to Jordan's older brother? Lucan was no more inclined to use his title than Jordan and Gideon were, but there was still no doubting that Lucan was every bit as arrogant as their aristocratic ducal forebears were reputed to have been!

'Yes, lucky for you,' Jordan agreed dryly. 'As for dinner—I believe you said that eating a healthy diet was a necessary part of my treatment?' he reminded her.

She smiled slightly. 'Do I take it from that comment that it's your intention to agree to accept only the parts of that treatment which suit you?'

'Of course.' He looked at her down his gorgeous nose.

Stephanie had never met anyone quite like Jordan St Claire.

Never before had she wanted to slap a man at the

same time as she so desperately wanted to experience the passion of his kisses!

She sighed. 'I'm afraid it doesn't work like that.'

'You aren't afraid at all, Stephanie,' he contradicted her flatly.

He had no idea! 'What work are you doing in your study?'

'None of your damned business,' Jordan said evenly.

So much for trying to change the subject to something less controversial!

The real problem for Stephanie was that even when they weren't engaged in one of these irritating conversations she was still aware of everything about him. Even sitting down and eating lunch with him had been something of an ordeal in self-restraint.

She had found herself looking at Jordan's hands far too often as he ate, easily able to remember those hands caressing her back earlier. Igniting that fire of longing inside her...

Oh, God! she thought, almost groaning aloud. Maybe she should just leave here, after all? Admit defeat and just go. Before she was tempted into doing something she would most definitely regret.

No, she *couldn't* leave.

Between the two of them, Richard and Rosalind Newman had been making Stephanie's life in London a living hell. She simply refused to let her awareness of Jordan force her into returning until Joey could assure her that particular nightmare was over.

'Is there anything you want me to pass on to Lucan when I speak to him later this afternoon?' She arched challenging brows.

Jordan scowled back at her. 'I very much doubt that

my big brother expects you to give him an hour-by-hour report on my progress.'

'Or otherwise,' she shot back.

'Or otherwise,' he confirmed

'No, probably not,' Stephanie accepted lightly. 'But as I have nothing else to do this afternoon...'

Jordan knew the little minx was challenging him. Attempting to hold the threat of Lucan's displeasure over him. A totally useless threat as far as Jordan was concerned. 'I ceased being in awe of my brother the moment I realised that he has to go to the bathroom like the rest of humanity.'

She grimaced. 'I really didn't need that image, thank you very much!'

Jordan shrugged. 'Believe me, it's a good leveller in almost any circumstances.'

'In Lucan's case, it's one I could well do without.'

'Suit yourself,' Jordan drawled. 'I usually like to eat dinner about seven.'

'When you bother to eat at all.'

He gave a mocking smile. 'As you've insisted on staying here, I expect to eat regularly and often.'

Stephanie wasn't totally sure which appetite Jordan was referring to, but she had her suspicions...

She had worked with dozens of patients over the last three years. Young. Old. Female as well as male. Some of them had been extremely difficult to work with, yes—those were the cases she specialised in, after all—but none of them had been as impossible as the man standing in front of her now.

Her mouth firmed. 'At the risk of repeating myself—I am not here for your amusement.'

'Repeat yourself all you like, Stephanie,' he said. 'The only things you can do for me at the moment are feed me or amuse me. I'll leave it up to you which one you want to do at any given time…'

Stephanie stared at him furiously for several seconds. 'Oh, just go away, will you?' she finally huffed irritably. In all of her daydreams, all her fantasies about actually meeting Jordan Simpson, Stephanie had never once imagined herself telling him to go away!

'I'll take that to mean that you want time to think about what to cook me for dinner,' Jordan said.

Stephanie shot him another frowning glare, only breathing a sigh of relief once he had left the kitchen. She heard the sound of him whistling tunelessly to himself as he walked down the corridor and then shut the study door behind him seconds later.

There *had* to be a way for Stephanie to get through to Jordan—to make him accept the professional help Lucan had hired her for. She just had no idea what it was!

'Comfortable?' Jordan asked sarcastically later that evening, as he entered the sitting room to find her curled up comfortably in one of the armchairs, the only illumination in the room coming from the warm and crackling fire she had lit in the hearth.

'Very, thank you,' she answered, and she sat up to swing her bare feet slowly to the floor, still wearing the dark green sweater and fitted jeans she had changed into earlier. 'It isn't seven o'clock yet, is it?'

Jordan's jaw tightened, and his eyes hooded to conceal their expression as he took in how the firelight picked out every amazing colour in Stephanie's plaited hair. 'I've worked long enough for now. How was your afternoon?' He leant heavily on his cane as he came further into the room, the pain in his hip and leg from sitting down all afternoon making his tone harsher than he'd intended.

'Boring,' she admitted.

He raised dark brows. 'Boring?'

She gave a shrug. 'I'm simply not used to sitting around all day having nothing to do.'

Boredom was something that Jordan knew a lot about, after the weeks he had spent in hospital in the States before coming here. 'There's lots of books in here you could have read. Or you could have gone for another walk. Or another swim,' he added dryly.

Stephanie gave a pained wince. 'I'm not going back in the pool until you do.'

'Then you'll be waiting a long time,' Jordan rasped, scowling as moved awkwardly to drop down into the armchair opposite hers, sighing in relief to be off his hip once again. He dropped his head back against the chair to turn and look at her. 'Do you ever wear your hair loose?'

Stephanie put a self-conscious hand up to the slightly untidy plait. 'Not really.'

'Then why bother to keep it long at all?'

'I— I've never really thought about it.' She frowned, very uncomfortable under the scrutiny of that piercingly narrowed gaze.

Jordan looked predatory in the firelight, his eyes an amber glitter, every sculptured angle of his face thrown into sharp relief: the harsh slash of his cheekbones, the long aristocratic nose, his hard, sensual mouth, and the strong lines of his jaw darkened by a five o'clock shadow.

Stephanie sensed a waiting stillness about him. A coiled expectancy much like a jungle cat poised to spring. With Stephanie as its prey!

She stood up abruptly, needing to escape from all that leashed power for a few minutes, at least. 'Would you like a glass of wine before dinner?'

Jordan gave a brief smile. 'I thought you would never ask.'

Stephanie paused in the doorway. 'You're in pain again, aren't you?' She could see by the deepening of the grooves beside his eyes and mouth and the weary droop of his head that he was inwardly battling to keep that pain under his control rather than letting it control him.

He shot her a hard look. 'Just get the damned wine, will you?'

She bit back her own angry retort, knowing by the dangerous glitter in Jordan's eyes that now was not the time to argue with him on the subject of the pain he was suffering. Or the unsatisfactory method he chose to dull that pain. 'Would you like red or white?'

'That all depends what you're making for dinner.'

She shrugged. 'I have potatoes and lasagne baking in the oven, and a salad made up and stored in the fridge.'

'Red, then. Just go, will you, Stephanie?' he urged fiercely as she still hesitated in the doorway. 'When you come back I promise to try and do my best to make polite pre-dinner conversation.' The harshness of his expression softened slightly.

She looked sceptical. 'About what?'

'How the hell should I know?' His snappy impatience wasn't in the least conducive to polite conversation! 'It's been so long since I tried that I think I've lost the art of small talk.'

Stephanie wasn't sure he'd ever had it!

Even as the charming and magnetically handsome

Jordan Simpson, he'd been known as a man who didn't suffer fools gladly—a professional perfectionist, with little patience for actors less inclined to give so completely of themselves.

As Jordan St Claire, a man well away from the public limelight, he didn't even attempt any of the social niceties, but was either caustic or mocking. That mood depended, Stephanie was fast realising, on the degree of pain he was in at the time. Right now she would say he was in a *lot* of pain.

'I've never particularly enjoyed the shallowness of small talk, either,' Stephanie told him.

'Then I guess we'll both have to work at it, won't we?' Jordan closed his eyes to lay his head back against the chair, his expression harsh and unapproachable.

Or just pained...

Stephanie was becoming more convinced by the moment that his hip and leg were more painful than usual this evening. She could see the effects of that pain in the dark shadows beneath those gold-coloured eyes, and in the way his skin stretched tautly over those high cheekbones and shadowed jaw. No doubt wine helped to numb that pain for a while, but it wouldn't take it away completely.

Even though she didn't think drinking wine was the answer, she knew that Jordan accepting some sort of help to manage his pain was better than no help at all. So she turned on her heel and sped off to get some.

'Here you are.' Stephanie returned from the kitchen a few minutes later to hand Jordan one of the glasses of red wine she'd brought, and placed the bottle on the table beside him before carrying her own glass across the room and resuming her seat near the warmth of the fire. 'So, what shall we talk about?' she prompted after a few minutes of awkward silence.

Jordan had sat up to drink half the glass of Merlot in one swallow, knowing from experience that it would take a few minutes for the alcohol to kick into his system and hopefully numb some of the pain in his hip and leg. 'Why don't you start by telling me about your family?' He refilled his glass as he waited for her to answer.

She raised surprised brows. 'What do you want to know about them?'

'You're really hard work, do you know that?' he growled.

'And you aren't?'

'You already know about my family,' Jordan pointed out. 'Two brothers, both older than me, one by two years, the other by two minutes. End of story.'

'What about your parents? Are they both still alive?' Stephanie sipped her own wine more slowly.

'Just my mother. She lives in Scotland,' Jordan answered curtly.

Stephanie seemed to expect him to say more on the subject. But Jordan had no intention of saying any more. He wasn't going to tell her that his mother, the Duchess of Stourbridge, was desperately awaiting the marriage of her eldest son so that she could step back and become simply the Dowager Duchess. That she was impatiently waiting for *any* of her sons to marry and provide her with the grandchildren she so longed for. As none of those three sons had ever had a permanent woman in his life, let alone thought of marriage, she was in for a very long wait indeed.

So instead Molly doted on her three sons. In fact if she had her way she would be down here right now, fussing over Jordan. Much as he loved and appreciated his mother, that was something he could definitely do without!

'Your turn,' he invited Stephanie dryly. 'Start with your grandparents and work your way down,' Jordan prompted as she hesitated.

She gave an awkward shrug. 'I don't usually discuss my private life with my patients.'

'I thought we had agreed that I'm not your patient?'

'Then what am I doing here?'

'Who the hell knows?' Jordan heard the aggression in his tone, and regretted it, but the wine was taking longer than usual to numb the pain this evening—to the point that he was gritting his teeth together so tightly he was surprised he could talk at all!

Stephanie gave him a reproving frown. 'Very well. All four of my grandparents are still alive. As are both my parents. I—'

'I wasn't asking for a roll call,' Jordan sighed. 'Look, Stephanie, this is how it goes, okay? I ask you a polite question, you give me a pleasant answer. With details. *Voilà*—small talk.'

Stephanie knew what small talk was. She just didn't have any patience for it. 'My paternal grandparents moved to Surrey when my grandfather sold his construction business five years ago. My maternal grandparents live in Oxfordshire—my grandmother is a retired university professor, and simply couldn't bring herself to move from the city where she had taught for so many years. My mother and father live in Kent and run a garden centre together.'

'Better.' Jordan nodded approvingly.

'I have one sibling. Joey. She—'

'Joey is a she?'

'Short for Josephine,' Stephanie supplied with a

smile, relieved to see that some of the pained tension was starting to leave Jordan's face. 'But anyone calling her by that name had better be prepared to receive a black eye or worse!'

'Worse?'

'She put a frog down the shirt of a boy at school when he dared to tease her by chanting her full name,' she remembered affectionately.

'And the black eye?'

'A man she dated for a while at university.' Stephanie shrugged. 'Needless to say they didn't date again after that.'

'No, I don't suppose they did,' Jordan chuckled softly as he felt his muscles starting to relax from the effects of the wine and the soothing firelight. 'So how old is Joey and what does she do?'

'She's a lawyer.'

'Aged…?'

'Late twenties,' Stephanie answered evasively before taking a sip of her own wine; she had known exactly where this conversation was going the moment Jordan asked to know about her family!

'Older or younger than you?'

'Slightly younger.'

Jordan gave her a considering glance, sensing there was something that Stephanie wasn't telling him. 'How much younger?' he prompted slowly.

Her eyes glittered in the firelight as she glared across at him. 'About five minutes!'

'Why, Stephanie,' Jordan murmured teasingly, 'does this mean that you're a twin, too?'

Her mouth thinned. 'Yes.'

'And are you identical?'

'Yes.'

Jordan's brows rose incredulously. 'You mean there are *two* of you with that unusual red and cinnamon-coloured hair, those flashing green eyes, a determined chin and an infuriatingly stubborn temperament?'

Those green eyes instantly flashed. 'I do *not* have a stubborn temperament!'

'And the grass isn't green or the sky blue,' he retorted.

'Sometimes they aren't!' she pointed out triumphantly.

'I'm sure that once in a blue moon you aren't stubborn, either,' Jordan jeered. He gave her a considering look. 'Let me guess—Joey has short red hair and tends to wear mainly dark business suits and silk blouses?'

Stephanie gasped. 'How could you possibly know that?

Jordan shrugged. 'For the same reason Gideon and I are completely unalike in our tastes—twin or not, no one really wants to be a clone of another person.'

'But you and Gideon aren't identical.'

'In colouring, no,' Jordan said. 'But we're the same height, and we have a similar facial structure.' He smiled. 'Maybe we should introduce your twin sister to my twin brother and see what happens? As they're both lawyers they already have something in common.'

Stephanie knew exactly what would happen if the fiercely independent and outspoken Joey ever met either of Jordan's arrogant older brothers: sparks would most definitely fly!

'Perhaps not,' Jordan acknowledged dryly, seeming to read her mind. 'Much as they sometimes annoy the hell out of me, I'm not sure I would want to wish that onto either of my brothers.'

Stephanie bristled. 'Meaning?'

'Meaning that having one stubborn McKinley sister

around is more than enough for any man.' He laughed huskily.

The wine had obviously relaxed Jordan. So much so that he was back to tormenting her. Making her less wary of his hair-trigger temper and more aware of the dizzying attraction of him that could be so utterly mesmerising.

Stephanie moistened dry lips as she stood up restlessly. 'I think I'll just go and check on dinner—'

Jordan reached out to grasp hold of her arm as she passed his chair, his fingers like steel bands about her wrist. 'There's nothing in the oven that will spoil, is there?'

She sincerely hoped that the sudden thundering of her heart at Jordan's touch wasn't echoed by the pulse beating beneath his fingers! 'Not really.' She swallowed hard. 'I just thought—'

'You think far too much, Steph. Why don't you just allow yourself to feel for a change?' he encouraged softly.

Stephanie was feeling too much already—that was the problem!

She could feel the strength of Jordan's fingers curled about her flesh, the firm caress of his thumb against that rapidly beating pulse in her inner wrist, the heat of those gold-coloured eyes on her moist and parted lips, then moving lower to her rising and falling breasts. Holding her captive. Drawing her into the deep well of sensuality she could feel rising between them…

'I believe I told you not to call me Steph,' she murmured breathily.

'Your lips have told me several things that aren't echoed by your body language,' he murmured as he placed his wine glass down onto the table. 'You obviously have feeding me well in hand, so perhaps now would be a good time for you to amuse me,' he suggested softly as he tugged firmly on her wrist.

Stephanie tried to resist that tug. And failed. Instead she overbalanced and toppled over the arm of the chair to end up sitting on Jordan's thighs as he took her into his waiting arms. 'Jordan, this is definitely *not* a good idea—'

'I'm all out of good ideas, Stephanie,' Jordan said gruffly. 'Let's go with a bad one, instead, hmm?' he encouraged, as his head began to lower towards hers. 'They're usually much more fun, anyway.'

Jordan was going to kiss her. More than kiss her, Stephanie knew as she became instantly mesmerised by the intensity of his gaze.

'Maybe we'll have more success with this sitting down,' he murmured throatily, his breath a warm caress against her parted lips.

Stephanie attempted one last appeal for sanity. 'Jordan, we really can't do this.'

'Oh, but we really can,' he muttered, and his lips finally claimed hers.

It was a slow and leisurely kiss as Jordan sipped and nibbled at Stephanie's lips, tasting her, tantalising her, encouraging her to reciprocate, groaning low in his throat when her arm finally moved up about his shoulders and she pulled him down to her so that she could kiss him back.

Jordan felt a surge down the length of his spine as her fingers became entangled in the darkness of his hair when the kiss deepened, lips tasting, teeth gently biting, tongues dueling. Stephanie was obviously feeling a desire that was echoed in the pulsing hardness of Jordan's thighs.

He shifted slightly in the chair, so that Stephanie lay back against the arm of the chair as his mouth left hers to trail sensuously down the long column of her throat, his tongue rasping across that silky flesh. She tasted of warmth and sunshine, the lightness of her perfume shadowed by the essence of sweet arousal. An arousal that reflected the hot demand rising inside Jordan to once again hear those panting little cries and breathy groans as he pleasured her.

His hand moved caressingly beneath the soft wool of her sweater as he continued to taste that creamy throat. Stephanie's skin was as smooth as silk and just as delicious. He touched. Cupped her breast. Gently squeezed the rosy-pink nipple and then stroked that sensitive tip. Pushed the softness of her jumper up and feasted his gaze on those small and perfect breasts before lowering his head and claiming one of those roused tips in the heat of his mouth.

'Jordan!' Stephanie's back arched into his caress even as she gasped at the intimacy.

His mouth reluctantly released her, his eyes hot and dark as he looked down at that plump and moist nipple. 'You're too delicious for me to stop, love,' he murmured admiringly, and he stroked his thumb lightly over that plumpness before turning his attention to its twin, his tongue circling rhythmically across that rosy nub before drawing it into his mouth deeply, hungrily.

Stephanie was totally lost to sensation, her hand cradling the back of Jordan's head as his tongue rasped skilfully across her swollen nipple. The rush of pleasure between her thighs moistened her, even as she felt herself ache for him to touch her there too…

Jordan's eyes glowed deeply gold as he raised his head and held her gaze with his. He unbuttoned the fastening on her jeans before slowing pulling down the zip to reveal the black lace panties she wore beneath.

Stephanie couldn't move, couldn't breathe, moaning softly as Jordan lowered his head. She felt the softness of his tongue circling her navel, increasing the heat between her thighs as he plunged into that sensitive indentation even as his hands moved up her ribcage to cup and squeeze her breasts, to capture the swollen nipples once again in a rolling caress.

She was on fire. Hot. Aching. Wet. Needing. Oh, God, needing…!

Jordan answered that need as one of his hands moved to lie flat against the skin just below her waist before moving lower, and then lower still, slipping easily beneath the lace of her panties to seek out the silky damp curls below.

Stephanie cried out as he drew one finger lightly over and around the already swollen nubbin nestled amongst those curls. Over and over again. Round and round. Touching. Pressing. A rhythmic caress that increased the pressure building deep inside her.

Her cries became shaky gasps as she felt herself approaching a climax. Her fingers dug painfully into Jordan's shoulders as his lips and tongue continued to arouse her breasts and pleasure built and built inside her, driving her higher and higher. But he seemed to know exactly when to stop the intensity of those caresses to hold her time and time again on the edge of that release.

'Please, Jordan!' Stephanie finally gasped. She was going insane with need. Immeasurable ecstasy was just beyond her reach.

Jordan's mouth pulled on her breast at the exact moment he slid one long and penetrating finger inside the hot moistness of her, quickly joined by a second, stretching her, widening her to accommodate that invasion, even as the soft pad of his thumb continued to caress her sensitive nubbin.

Stephanie became so wet, so swollen, and those long fingers continued to plunge into her rhythmically, again and again, faster, harder, until the caresses pushed her over the edge into a climax so deep and prolonged it totally took her breath away and she could only cling onto him as she moved her hips into the burning intensity of that pulsing pleasure.

Jordan continued his caresses long after she had climaxed, the hardness of his own arousal continuing to pulse to the same rhythm as the echoing quivers still shaking her inside, and threatening to cause him to self-combust.

He had never been a selfish lover, finding as much satisfaction in giving his partner pleasure as he did in his own, and so he ignored the pulsing of his own body now to continue those caresses, wanting—needing—to give Stephanie every last vestige of physical pleasure.

He was less pleased with the sudden look of panicked awareness that widened those beautiful green eyes minutes later, as she returned to full awareness of where she was and what had just happened between them. 'It's okay, Steph,' he reassured her huskily.

'It is *not* okay!' she groaned self-consciously.

'Believe me, it is,' he soothed, even as he slowly, carefully, disengaged his fingers from her quivering flesh before refastening her jeans and pulling her sweater down. But not before he had given in to the temptation to gently kiss the slight redness of her breasts, where the stubble of his day's growth of beard had rubbed against that delicate skin.

He would have to shave twice a day if he wanted to do this again; he hated seeing even the slightest blemish on that perfect creamy skin.

His gaze was hooded when he finally looked up, to see that her face was flushed and her eyes fever-bright with uncertainty. 'You were beautiful, Stephanie,' he told her.

Her eyes were wide as she moistened dry lips with the tip of her little pink tongue. 'I— What about you? You didn't—'

'We have all night,' Jordan cut in as his hands moved gently from her breast to her thigh.

Her frown was pained. 'We really shouldn't—'

'We really *should*,' he insisted firmly.

She shook her head, her gaze not quite meeting his. 'I'm not sure I'll be able to stay on here if this is going to happen.'

Jordan's arms tightened about her as she struggled to stand up. 'Stay, Stephanie. Please.'

She looked up at him shyly. 'But—'

'If I had known you wanted to be alone, Jord, then I would have just telephoned you instead of flying up here to speak to you in person!' a mocking voice drawled behind them.

Jordan didn't need to turn and look across the room in order to know that the voice belonged to his twin brother Gideon…

CHAPTER SEVEN

'OH, GOD!' Stephanie gave a devastated groan and buried her heated cheeks against Jordan's chest after shooting a single glance across the room and seeing the devastatingly handsome blond-haired, dark-eyed man who stood in the open doorway, looking back at her with a cynical expression on his face.

'Not quite,' the man said derisively.

'Not even close, Gideon,' Jordan retorted.

'I guess you were a little too…preoccupied to hear the helicopter landing fifteen minutes ago?' Gideon said pointedly.

'I guess we were,' Jordan said acerbically. 'Does that mean that Lucan is here, too?' The scowl could be heard in his tone.

'I flew myself up.'

'Why?'

There was a short, telling pause. 'I would rather we talked in private, Jordan.'

'Not yet,' Jordan said grimly, his arms tightening about Stephanie as she trembled against him. 'How about giving the two of us a few minutes' privacy, Gideon?'

'By all means,' the other man murmured. 'Would you like me to continue waiting in the kitchen or—?'

'Will you just go, Gid?' Jordan grated harshly, and Stephanie gave another groan as she burrowed even deeper against his chest.

Stephanie wanted to die of embarrassment! She had never felt quite so much like crawling away and digging a hole before burying herself in it! She had done some stupid things in her life, but surely never anything quite so stupid as this?

Not only had she become totally lost in Jordan's kisses and caresses, but there had been a witness to that loss of control. Not just any witness, either, but obviously Jordan's twin brother!

'It's okay, Stephanie, he's gone; you can come out now,' Jordan cajoled.

Gideon St Claire might indeed have left the room, but Jordan certainly hadn't. And Stephanie was no more eager to look *him* in the face again after what had just happened than she was his brother.

What on earth had possessed her to behave in that totally uninhibited way?

With Jordan Simpson, of all men!

She had no choice now—no more arguments to make to the contrary. She had to leave. Immediately. She couldn't stay on here another minute, another second—

'Stephanie, calm down!' Jordan ordered as she sat up and began to struggle for release from his restraining arms. 'We're both consenting adults and— Damn it, Stephanie, we haven't done anything wrong.'

Stephanie stopped struggling long enough to glare up at him. '*You* may not have done, but *I* certainly have!' She gave a self-disgusted shake of her head, eyes huge in the pallor of her face. 'I have to leave right now, Jordan.'

'Why do you?' His arms tightened about her. 'Gideon never stays long.'

'As far as I'm concerned he's been here far too long already!' Her eyes flashed with the glitter of the emeralds they resembled as she glared up at him. 'Let go of me,' she pleaded, as she attempted to stand up and found the tightening of Jordan's arms once again prevented her from doing so.

His jaw was clenched. 'Not until you calm down.'

Stephanie *was* calm. Or as calm as she was ever going to be when she had just made a complete idiot of herself. Not just with Jordan, but in front of his brother too…

Stephanie inwardly cringed as she thought of how intimately Jordan had touched her. How completely unravelled she had become under the influence of those caresses. How her body, her breasts, were still so highly sensitised she could feel the brush of her clothing against her skin. How the heat of her thighs still quaked and trembled in the aftermath of that earth-shattering climax!

Jordan shrugged. 'I accept it was a little inconvenient, having Gideon walk in on us like that, but—'

'A little inconvenient?' Stephanie gave a humourless laugh as she finally managed to wrench herself out of Jordan's arms and surged forcefully to her feet, straightening and fastening her clothing before turning back to glower down at him. 'How long do you think your brother was standing there? Do you think that he saw—that he heard—?' She broke off with a groan as she thought of the way she had cried out loud as those powerful waves of release had surged through her.

Jordan shook his head. 'Even if Gideon did see or

hear anything, I assure you he's too much of a gentleman ever to mention it.'

'You're just making the situation worse, Jordan!' Stephanie said in protest, and raised her hands to the heat of her cheeks.

Jordan could see that as far as Stephanie was concerned that was exactly what he was doing. But, while he accepted that it was a little awkward to have had Gideon walk in on them in that way, he didn't consider it quite as cataclysmic as Stephanie seemed to. 'Look, just put it to the back of your mind—'

'That's easy for you to say when you weren't the one caught in a compromising position!'

Jordan watched as Stephanie began to agitatedly pace the room, obviously unaware that her hair had come loose during their lovemaking and now fell in a fiery cascade about her shoulders, the firelight picking out the gold and cinnamon highlights amongst the fiery red.

She looked beautiful. Wild and wanton. Like a woman who had just been thoroughly made love to. Only not quite as thoroughly as he'd have liked!

'Oh, I'm pretty sure that I was there too,' he pointed out, the tightening throbbing of his arousal a sharp reminder that he hadn't attained that same release.

Her eyes narrowed to icy-green slits. 'I should warn you, Jordan, I'm not in the mood right now to appreciate your warped sense of humour.'

'Then stop making such a big deal out of this,' he snapped, his expression grim as he reached for his cane and rose awkwardly to his feet. It eased the confines of his painfully engorged arousal, if nothing else!

'It *is* a big deal, damn it!' Stephanie said emotionally. 'Not only do I not normally behave in that—that

Get 2 Books FREE!

Harlequin® Books,
publisher of women's fiction,
presents

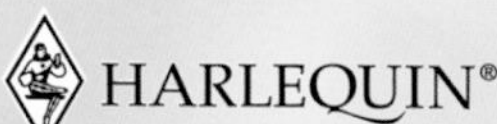

Presents®

FREE BOOKS! Use the reply card inside to get two free books!

FREE GIFTS! You'll also get two exciting surprise gifts, absolutely free!

GET 2 BOOKS

We'd like to send you two *Harlequin Presents*® novels absolutely free. Accepting them puts you under no obligation to purchase any more books.

HOW TO GET YOUR 2 FREE BOOKS AND 2 FREE GIFTS

1. Return the reply card today, and we'll send you two *Harlequin Presents* novels, absolutely free! We'll even pay the postage!
2. Accepting free books places you under no obligation to buy anything, ever. Whatever you decide, the free books and gifts are yours to keep, free!
3. We hope that after receiving your free books you'll want to remain a subscriber, but the choice is yours—to continue or cancel, any time at all!

EXTRA BONUS

You'll also get two free mystery gifts! (worth about $10)

® and ™ are trademarks owned and used by the trademark owner and/or its licensee.
© 2010 HARLEQUIN ENTERPRISES LIMITED. Printed in the U.S.A.

FREE!

Return this card today to get
2 FREE BOOKS and 2 FREE GIFTS!

HARLEQUIN®

YES! Please send me 2 FREE *Harlequin Presents®* novels, and 2 free mystery gifts as well. I understand I am under no obligation to purchase anything, as explained on the back of this insert.

About how many NEW paperback fiction books have you purchased in the past 3 months?

❑ 0-2 E7RQ ❑ 3-6 E7SQ ❑ 7 or more E7S2

☐ I prefer the regular-print edition 106/306 HDL ☐ I prefer the larger-print edition 176/376 HDL

FIRST NAME LAST NAME

ADDRESS

APT.# CITY

STATE/PROV. ZIP/POSTAL CODE

Visit us at: www.ReaderService.com

Offer limited to one per household and not applicable to series that subscriber is currently receiving. **Your Privacy**—The Reader Service is committed to protecting your privacy. Our Privacy Policy is available online at www.ReaderService.com or upon request from the Reader Service. We make a portion of our mailing list available to reputable third parties that offer products we believe may interest you. If you prefer that we not exchange your name with third parties, or if you wish to clarify or modify your communication preferences, please visit us at www.ReaderService.com/consumerschoice or write to us at Reader Service Preference Service, P.O. Box 9062, Buffalo, NY 14269. Include your complete name and address.

▶ DETACH AND MAIL CARD TODAY! ▶

(H-P-04/11)

The Reader Service - Here's how it works:

Accepting your 2 free books and 2 free mystery gifts (mystery gifts worth approximately $10.00) places you under no obligation to buy anything. You may keep the books and gifts and return the shipping statement marked "cancel". If you do not cancel, about a month later we'll send you 6 additional books and bill you just $4.05 each for the regular-print edition or $4.55 each for the larger-print edition in the U.S. or $4.74 each for the regular-print edition or $5.24 each for the larger-print edition in Canada. That is a savings of at least 13% off the cover price. It's quite a bargain! Shipping and handling is just 50¢ per book in the U.S. and 75¢ per book in Canada.* You may cancel at any time, but if you choose to continue, every month we'll send you 6 more books, which you may either purchase at the discount price or return to us and cancel your subscription.

*Terms and prices subject to change without notice. Prices do not include applicable taxes. Sales tax applicable in N.Y. Canadian residents will be charged applicable taxes. Offer not valid in Quebec. All orders are subject to credit approval. Credit or debit balances in a customer's account(s) may be offset by any other outstanding balance owed by or to the customer. Books received may not be as shown. Please allow 4 to 6 weeks for delivery. Offer valid while quantities last.

If offer card is missing, write to: The Reader Service, P.O. Box 1867, Buffalo, NY 14240-1867 or visit www.ReaderService.com

NO POSTAGE
NECESSARY
IF MAILED
IN THE
UNITED STATES

BUSINESS REPLY MAIL

FIRST-CLASS MAIL PERMIT NO. 717 BUFFALO, NY

POSTAGE WILL BE PAID BY ADDRESSEE

THE READER SERVICE
PO BOX 1867
BUFFALO NY 14240-9952

abandoned way, but I certainly don't do it in front of an audience.'

'I told you—Gideon won't refer to it again if you don't.'

'As if I ever want to *think* about it again, let alone talk about it!' Stephanie exclaimed.

Jordan's mouth tightened and he suddenly became very still. 'Why is that, exactly?' His voice was silky soft. Deadly.

'Why?' she repeated incredulously.

'Yes—why?'

'Surely it's *obvious*?'

A nerve pulsed in Jordan's tightly clenched jaw. 'You wanted it. I wanted it. And as I said we're both well over the age of consent—so what's your problem?' he snarled.

'My problem is that Lucan hired me to be your physiotherapist, not to go to bed with you,' she told him heatedly.

'I don't need a physiotherapist—'

'Oh, yes you do—'

'And we didn't go anywhere near a bed,' Jordan continued coldly.

He just wasn't getting this, Stephanie realised impatiently. And why should he? Gideon was his brother, and if his closeness to his twin was anything like her own to Joey, then Jordan felt none of the awkwardness at his brother's intrusion into their lovemaking that Stephanie did. But then, he wasn't the one who had totally lost control. Who had screamed in ecstasy as he found release—

Oh, God, Jordan's hands had been all over her body! *In* her body!

Stephanie sat down abruptly in one of the armchairs,

putting her hands completely over the heat of her face as she felt the tears well up before falling hotly down her cheeks.

Jordan stared down in utter frustration at Stephanie's bent head as he heard her quiet sobs, having absolutely no idea what he should do or say next. In his experience women didn't usually cry after he had made love to them!

They didn't usually cry after they had made love with world-famous actor Jordan *Simpson*, he reminded himself grimly; the crippled, useless Jordan St Claire was obviously something else entirely. Some*one* else entirely!

God, how he hated feeling so damned helpless. So unlike himself. It was—

'I've been thinking…'

Jordan turned fiercely at the sound of his brother's voice. 'Get *out* of here, Gideon!'

'That I'm probably an unwanted third,' his brother finished unhurriedly, and gave a pointed look in the direction of the obviously upset Stephanie. 'I can easily book into the pub in the village for the night and come back in the morning.'

'No!' Stephanie looked up to protest, hastily drying her cheeks as she stood up. 'Of course you mustn't leave, Mr St Claire—'

'Gideon,' he invited coolly. 'Mr St Claire makes me sound too much like my older brother.'

'Whatever,' she dismissed uncomfortably. 'You have as much right to stay here as Jordan does. I'm the one who should leave.'

'Oh, I doubt my baby brother would be too happy about that,' Gideon said, after a swift glance in Jordan's direction.

The two brothers were like two sides of a negative, Stephanie suddenly realized: Jordan's hair was long and dark, whereas his brother's was the colour of gold and styled ruthlessly short. Jordan's eyes were the same gold as his brother's hair, and Gideon's eyes were so dark and hard they appeared almost black. And the contrast in the way they were dressed was just as extreme. Jordan's clothes were casual; Gideon St Claire wore tailored black trousers and a black cashmere sweater over a grey shirt unbuttoned at the throat, his black leather shoes obviously handmade.

They were also two of the most devastatingly handsome men Stephanie had ever set eyes on!

'You're right. He *wouldn't* like that,' Jordan answered his brother. 'Let's get the introductions over with and go on from there, shall we?' he suggested. 'Stephanie, meet my brother Gideon St Claire. Gideon, this is Stephanie McKinley.'

Stephanie didn't know quite what to make of the fact that he didn't add anything else to his introduction to explain what she was actually doing there. Although *she* didn't feel too inclined to explain what she was doing there to the haughty Gideon St Claire, either, after the intimacy of the scene he had walked in on only minutes ago!

'Mr St Claire,' she said with a stiff nod.

'Miss McKinley,' he murmured, his features every bit as hard and chiselled as his twin's.

Stephanie had no doubt this cynically tough man was a formidable lawyer. She would have to ask Joey if she had ever met him in court…

'McKinley…?' Gideon St Claire repeated slowly, his dark gaze narrowing on her in shrewd assessment. 'Red hair. Green eyes. Hmm.' His mouth compressed. 'You wouldn't happen to be related to Josephine McKinley, would you?' he asked.

Oh, dear Lord! Stephanie's sister and this man *had* met. But when? And where? Please, please, God, let it not be in any way connected with the Newmans' pending divorce case!

Just thinking of Jordan's reaction if he learned that she was being named as the 'other woman' in a divorce—albeit falsely—after the disgust he had shown for his own father's infidelity, was enough to make her feel ill.

'Her twin.' Jordan was the one to answer his brother—economically. 'And apparently she hates to be called Josephine,' he added.

'Do you know my sister, Mr St Claire?' Stephanie eyed Gideon warily.

'Not personally, no,' he said. 'I have heard of her, though,' he added.

And nothing good, either, if the hard glitter in those piercing dark eyes and the contemptuous curl of those sculptured lips was any indication!

Stephanie knew that Joey had earned herself something of a reputation in the courts of law these last three years, and that many of her colleagues considered her to be ruthless and uncompromising in defence of her clients. Character traits Stephanie would have thought a man like Gideon St Claire, who so obviously possessed those same traits himself, would have appreciated.

'What are you doing here, Gideon?' Jordan demanded—and thankfully saved Stephanie from having to make any sort of reply to his twin's enigmatic comment about her sister!

Instead of answering his brother, Gideon turned

those cool, dark eyes on Stephanie. 'I thought I smelt something burning when I was in the kitchen…'

'The lasagne!' Stephanie wailed as she remembered the food she had left cooking in the oven earlier. Before Jordan had begun making love to her and she had forgotten all about it! 'Excuse me.' She shot the two men a bright, meaningless smile before hurrying from the room.

It was patently obvious that Gideon wanted to talk to Jordan alone, and Stephanie was glad of an excuse to escape the intensity of emotion in being in the presence of two of the arrogantly overwhelming St Claire brothers.

'Well, you've succeeded in effectively getting Stephanie out of the room, so now you can tell me what's going on,' Jordan prompted as soon as he and Gideon were alone in the sitting room.

Gideon gazed back at him with the cynical speculation that was so characteristic of him. So typical of all three of the St Claire brothers, if he were totally honest, Jordan acknowledged ruefully; their father really did have a lot more to answer for than just hurting their mother.

Gideon gave a rueful shake of his head. 'And I've been imagining you all alone in the wilds of Gloucestershire.'

Jordan grimaced. 'I know your sarcasm usually manages to put the fear of God into most people, Gid, but I assure you I'm not one of them.' He dropped wearily back into the armchair he had only recently vacated.

'You look like hell!' his brother declared as he looked down at him with harsh disapproval.

'As complimentary as ever,' Jordan murmured, and rested his head tiredly against the chair.

He had forgotten all about the pain in his hip and leg—just as Stephanie had obviously forgotten about dinner—while the two of them were making love, but now that that rush of adrenaline had subsided Jordan once again felt the grinding and remorseless ache in his right thigh and down his leg.

Maybe he should go back to the States and see one of the specialists, as Stephanie had advised he should do?

No, damn it. He would rather live with the pain than suffer any more of those unhelpful medical examinations!

'Have they run out of razors in Gloucestershire?' Gideon raised enquiring brows.

'Just tell me what you're doing here, Gideon,' Jordan said again irritably, wondering why the hell it was that everyone was suddenly so obsessed with his appearance. What did it matter what he looked like when there was no one here to see him? Well…until Stephanie had arrived yesterday. And now Gideon, too. 'Well?' He glared at his brother.

'I certainly had no intention of interrupting your little assignation with La McKinley,' his brother retorted as he moved to fold his lean length into the chair opposite Jordan's.

'It isn't an assignation,' Jordan denied wearily.

'No?'

'Look at me, Gideon.' He sighed heavily. 'I'm just a shell of the man I used to be.'

'Stephanie doesn't seem to mind,' his brother pointed out.

Jordan's eyes narrowed warningly. 'Perhaps we should just leave Stephanie out of this.'

Gideon glanced in the direction of the kitchen. 'She doesn't seem like your usual type of woman…'

'As I just said, I'm not my usual self!' Jordan snapped back.

'Aren't you a little tired of wallowing in self-pity?' Gideon asked.

That remark was so reminiscent of the one Stephanie had made to Jordan yesterday that it totally infuriated him. In fact, if Gideon had been anyone else Jordan knew he would have given in to the urge he felt to get up and punch him on his arrogant nose! As it was, he knew that Gideon was more than capable of besting him in any fight at the moment—verbal or physical.

Not that Jordan was fooled for a moment by Gideon's seemingly hard and unsympathetic attitude; as his brother—his twin—Jordan knew how devastated Gideon had been following the accident. He also knew that his brother was a man of strong emotions—he just preferred to keep them hidden most of the time, behind a mask of cynicism.

'Just stop trying to annoy me and get on with it, Gid,' he said.

Thankfully Stephanie had managed to salvage the lasagne from the oven before it was totally ruined. A little trimming round the edges had disposed of the worst of the burnt pasta, and the potatoes were still edible too.

By the time the two St Claire men joined her in the kitchen ten minutes later she had laid three places at the table and was ready to serve the food. Whether or not Stephanie would actually be able to sit down with them and eat any of it was another matter entirely!

The ten minutes' respite from both Jordan's disturbing company and that of his coldly remote brother had at least given Stephanie a chance to regain some of her composure, although she still felt ill every time she so much as thought of making love with Jordan.

Or, more accurately, Jordan making love to her.

She wasn't a complete innocent when it came to love-making; she had dated and experimented a little when she was at university and found it all extremely disappointing. So much so that Stephanie had spared little time for relationships since then, and had concentrated on her career instead. Her physical response to Jordan had been far from disappointing—in fact it had been as combustible as it had been instantaneous. She had never dreamed, never imagined—not even in her wildest fantasies—the pleasure she had felt when Jordan made love to her.

Which was traumatic enough in itself, without having Jordan's coldly cynical twin—the man of whom Jordan had warned Stephanie she didn't know what arrogance was until she'd met him—as witness to that complete physical unravelling.

Not that there was any evidence of that knowledge in the remoteness of Gideon's expression now, as he entered the kitchen behind Jordan. 'I apologise once again for causing you any inconvenience, Stephanie,' he said politely as he saw the three places laid at the table.

'Not at all,' she dismissed brightly. 'After all, your family owns this estate. Now, there's more than enough food here for three— Are you all right, Jordan?' she asked with concern, as she noticed how pale he was. Worse than pale. His cheeks actually had a slightly grey cast to them. And was it her imagination or did he seem to be leaning more heavily on his cane than usual?

Was it as a result of having made love to her?

Jordan might be sarcastic and mocking, but he was also obviously still far from well—something that any excess of physical activity was sure to exacerbate. Making love could definitely be classed as excessive physical activity—especially as she'd been cuddled up on his lap!

She moved swiftly to his side. 'Perhaps you should sit down—'

'Would you stop fussing over me like some mother hen?' He turned on her savagely, eyes glittering deeply gold in warning.

Stephanie drew back sharply at his tone. 'Sorry.' She grimaced. 'I just thought—'

'Haven't I already told you that you think too damned much?' He scowled down at her.

'I trust you will excuse my brother's rudeness, Stephanie?' Gideon cut into the exchange with disapproving coldness. 'The discomfort of his injuries seems to have robbed him of his manners.'

'When I want you to apologise for me, Gid, I'll ask!' Jordan said furiously.

'When I want you to tell me what to do and when to do it, then *I'll* ask, Jord,' his brother came back with heavy sarcasm.

At any other time Stephanie would have found this challenging conversation between two obviously well-matched and determined men amusing. But as she had earlier almost made love with one of them, and been literally caught in the act by the second, Stephanie wasn't in any frame of mind at that moment to find anything either of them did in the least amusing!

Especially when Jordan already looked as if he were on the point of collapse… 'I really think you should sit down, Jordan,' she told him firmly, and she pointedly drew back one of the kitchen chairs before looking up at him expectantly.

Jordan shot her a narrow-eyed glare, more aware than ever of his own limitations when in the company of his brother's lean and healthy frame. Just as he was aware of the appraising looks Gideon was giving Stephanie as he watched her from beneath hooded lids…

Jordan slowly lowered himself down onto the wooden chair. 'Pack your bag once we've had dinner, Stephanie,' he told her tersely as he turned to place his cane conveniently against the wall behind him. 'Gideon is going to fly us all back to London in the helicopter early tomorrow morning.'

'I— What…?' Stephanie made no effort to hide her total bewilderment at Jordan's sudden announcement.

'We're all going back to London. In the morning,' Jordan repeated with ill-concealed impatience.

'But what about my car?'

'I'll arrange for someone to come and collect it,' he dismissed.

'But—why…?'

'Does it matter why?' Jordan snapped.

'Well…no, I suppose not…' Stephanie gave a slightly dazed shake of her head.

Except that Stephanie didn't *want* to be back in London; she had taken this job in Gloucestershire with Jordan St Claire for the very reason that she had wanted to get away from London and stay away—until her unwilling involvement in the Newmans' impending divorce had been effectively dealt with!

CHAPTER EIGHT

'WHAT is it, Stephanie?'

She stood hesitantly in the doorway of the study, where Jordan once again sat behind the imposing desk looking at her with enigmatic eyes. The only light in the room came from the lamp on top of the desk, reflecting down onto the papers he was working on.

As expected, as far as Stephanie was concerned, sitting down and eating dinner with the St Claire brothers had been an uncomfortable experience. She had absolutely no idea how the two men had felt about it. Conversation had been virtually non-existent as they'd both eaten in brooding silence, obviously lost in their own thoughts. Although Gideon *had* politely thanked and complimented Stephanie on the food once they had all finished eating, before excusing himself and going upstairs to bed.

Stephanie had a feeling his early departure might have had more to do with feeling that 'unwanted third' he'd mentioned than an actual need to go to bed. He had probably retired early because he thought that Jordan and Stephanie needed some privacy—if only to discuss leaving tomorrow.

If that were the case, then Gideon could have saved himself the trouble. Because Jordan had abruptly excused himself too, and disappeared off to his study only a minute or so after his brother's departure. Leaving Stephanie with far too much time on her hands to remember and cringe at her earlier behaviour…

She gave a non-committal shrug now. 'As you intend leaving with Gideon in the morning, it might be as well if we were to say goodbye now.'

Jordan straightened to narrow his speculative gaze on her. 'I'm sure I made it more than plain that I expect you to accompany us to London.'

'Yes, you did.' Stephanie stepped further into the room. 'But you've also made it clear since my arrival here that you don't want the attentions of a physiotherapist. As such, this would be the ideal opportunity for me to—'

'Have you been thinking again, Stephanie?' he taunted softly as he relaxed back against the leather chair.

'Stop it, Jordan!' She eyed him cautiously as she moved to stand in front of the desk. 'Obviously I will need to contact Lucan and let him know that as I never actually started working with you I won't be requiring any payment—'

'I'm sure that's very fair of you, Stephanie,' Jordan cut in. 'But as far as I'm aware Lucas has not yet suggested dispensing with your services.'

'No.' She sighed. 'But it's been pretty much a non-starter from the beginning, so I assumed—'

'It never pays to make assumptions about the St Claire family, Stephanie.' Jordan shook his head even as his mouth thinned. 'When I said we're *all* going back to London in the morning, Stephanie, that's exactly what I meant.'

She frowned. 'I can't see what possible point there

would be in accompanying you when you refuse to let me do anything to help you.'

'Maybe I've reconsidered?'

Stephanie looked across at him searchingly, but found herself unable to read anything from Jordan's deliberately closed expression and the enigmatic blankness in those gold-coloured eyes. 'Jordan—'

'Stephanie, Gideon flew here to let me know that my mother has arrived in London,' Jordan announced flatly.

'Oh?'

'Yes,' he bit out curtly. 'As she rarely leaves Edinburgh, that fact is significant in itself. So much so that Lucan decided to try and find out exactly why she's in London. He's managed to discover that she has an appointment to see a cancer specialist the day after tomorrow.' Jordan spoke heavily, still having trouble accepting the reason Gideon had flown up here in person to talk to him.

The three brothers' relationship with their father had been sporadic at best after their parents' separation and divorce, with none of them in any doubt as to who was to blame for the breakdown of the marriage. But their mother—their mother had always been there for all of them. Molly loved without wanting to possess, without judging. She never pushed. She cajoled. She never forced her own views onto any of her sons but instead encouraged them to make their own decisions and choices. And if any of those choices should be the wrong ones then she was there for them. Always.

Now it was time for them to be there for her...

'I'm so sorry.' Stephanie had moved to sit down on a chair on the opposite side of the desk.

'Nothing's certain yet,' Jordan said. 'It's a preliminary examination and may amount to nothing.'

'But…'

'Exactly. *But…'* He nodded grimly. 'Strange, isn't it?' he mused. 'How learning that someone you love may be seriously ill can shake you out of what Gideon—and incidentally you too—call wallowing in self-pity!'

Stephanie's cheeks coloured hotly. 'I only said that because—'

'Because it happens to be the truth,' Jordan said honestly as he stood to pick up his cane and begin restlessly pacing the room. 'My mother was the first member of the family to arrive in LA when I had my accident. She stayed at my bedside the whole time I was in hospital, and then again at my apartment for weeks afterwards. Always encouraging. Always positive. And all the time this damned thing was eating away at her.'

'You said nothing is certain yet,' Stephanie reminded him softly as she watched him pace.

'It's enough that the possibility is there.' Jordan's expression became even grimmer. 'We're going back to London tomorrow, Stephanie, and once we know exactly what's happening with my mother you're going to help me get my full health back.'

Stephanie couldn't have been more pleased that Jordan was at last willing to consider therapy on his leg and hip—although she might have wished the circumstances for making his decision had been different—but she was no longer sure she was the person to help him do it.

She had allowed herself to become personally involved with Jordan. More than just personally involved with him on a physical level. She didn't even want to *think* about what she might feel for him on an emotional one!

Except, she realised, that she already felt something…

Later, Stephanie, she instructed herself firmly. There would be plenty of opportunity once she and Jordan had said goodbye for her to analyse her feelings for him.

'That's wonderful, Jordan,' she said with approval. 'I'm more than happy to recommend another physiotherapist to you.'

'I don't want another physiotherapist, damn it!' Jordan growled as he came to stand in front of her. 'Stephanie?' He bent down slightly to place a hand beneath her chin and tilt her face up to his. 'Look at me!' he barked as her gaze avoided meeting his.

Stephanie looked up, and then as quickly glanced away again as she found herself unable to meet the intensity of that golden gaze. She shook her head. 'You must see—understand—that I can't possibly work with you now, Jordan.' Just the touch of his fingers against her chin was enough to reawaken all that earlier arousal. She longed for his hand to be touching more than her chin…

'Are you asking for my word that what happened earlier won't happen again?' he rasped. He shook his head. 'I can't give that. Can you?'

She moistened dry lips before answering him huskily, 'No. Which is my whole point,' she continued, before Jordan could comment. 'I can't possibly work with a man I've— A man who—' Stephanie groaned. She couldn't even say the words. 'I don't get personally involved with my patients, Jordan.'

He frowned down at her, making no effort to hide his frustration with her continued stubbornness.

Having made his decision to stop wallowing and actually do something about his leg, he wasn't willing to simply let Stephanie recommend someone else and then walk away from him.

Lucan only ever employed the best person there was for any particular job—which meant that Stephanie McKinley had to be the best physiotherapist the St Claire millions could buy. If Jordan was going to get back on both his feet, then the best was what he needed.

And it was *all* that he needed from Stephanie right now...

He released her chin abruptly and stepped back. 'I don't believe we *are* personally involved.'

She blinked. 'But earlier—'

'Forget earlier,' he advised icily. 'It never happened. I've just been playing with you,' he added. 'From now on we'll concentrate on what you really came here to do.'

Forget earlier. It never happened. I've just been playing with you...

It was the last of those statements that hurt Stephanie the most. Because she knew it was the truth? Or because it was already too late for her not to be emotionally involved with him?

A lot of good it would do her if she were!

At the moment Jordan St Claire was a man who had become out of touch with his real charming self as well as the life he had led before the accident. The A-list actor Jordan Simpson wouldn't even have looked at Stephanie McKinley twice. In fact he probably wouldn't have bothered looking at her once! And when Jordan was back on two healthy legs—

'Are you going to help me or not, Stephanie?'

He wouldn't look at her again, Stephanie finished with painful honesty.

She had initially taken this job with absolutely no doubt as to her professional ability to help Lucan St Claire's brother. The fact that the brother had turned out to be Jordan Simpson had complicated things from the beginning. That Stephanie's attraction to him had allowed things between them to go as awry as they had was more than a complication.

So, was she now going to let her emotions stand in the way of giving Jordan the help he needed? Was she going to deny him that help when he had finally asked her for it?

Stephanie knew she couldn't do that. Her professional dedication simply wouldn't allow it.

'Yes, Jordan, I'm sure I can help you.' She nodded as she stood up. She only hoped it was true. Just as she hoped that she could put away her personal feelings for this man and concentrate on helping him regain full health. 'Although I'm not too sure about flying to London in a helicopter,' she added with a grimace. She found flying in a normal plane traumatic enough, so goodness knew how she would feel in a flimsy helicopter.

He chuckled softly. 'We'll be quite safe with Gideon—he flies the same way he does everything. With icy reserve,' he supplied as Stephanie gave him a curious glance.

'I thought his earlier coolness was because he disapproved of me.' After all, he'd had reason enough to disapprove after the scene he had almost walked in on!

'No.' Jordan gave a humourless smile. 'You're no

exception to the rule, Stephanie—Gideon makes a point of disapproving of everyone.'

The three St Claire men were totally different from any other men she had ever met, Stephanie mused minutes later as she made her way up the stairs to bed. Lucan was cold and arrogant. Gideon icily reserved. Jordan—

Perhaps she had better not think any more about what sort of man Jordan was!

She especially shouldn't think about his recent admission that he had just been playing with her earlier on…

Jordan was seated in the front of the helicopter beside Gideon as they took off. Instinct alone made him glance back at Stephanie, only to realise that she had a death-grip on the arms of her own seat, her short fingernails digging into the leather.

'Are you okay?' he asked with concern.

She didn't even glance at him but continued to stare straight ahead, her eyes wide in a face that was completely devoid of colour, her jaw clenched as she spoke between gritted teeth. 'Fine.'

'No, you're not,' Jordan contradicted flatly as he undid his seat-belt. 'Keep it steady, Gideon,' he warned as he began to climb into the back.

'What are you doing?' Stephanie's expression was one of complete panic as Jordan's movements redistributed the weight and made the helicopter tilt slightly from side to side.

'Coming to sit next to you,' Jordan explained patiently as he sat down and buckled himself into the seat. Then he reached out and prised the fingers closest to him from the armrest, before taking Stephanie's hand firmly into his own. 'You don't like flying.' He stated the obvious.

'Hate it!' she muttered as her fingers tightened painfully about his. 'No criticism of your capabilities intended, Gideon,' she added shakily.

'None taken, I assure you,' he drawled confidently from the front of the aircraft.

Jordan ignored his brother's insouciance and concentrated on Stephanie. 'Why the hell didn't you tell me you don't like flying?'

She flashed him a green-eyed glare before hastily resuming her death-stare towards the front of the helicopter. 'I did tell you last night that I wasn't sure about flying in a helicopter!'

'Not sure and terrified are two distinctly different things!'

'What difference would it have made if I had been more forceful about it?' she snapped.

'We could have let Gideon fly back on his own and driven down.'

Stephanie shook her head, and then obviously regretted it as even her lips seemed to go white. 'You needed to get to London as quickly as possible.' Her jaw was once again tightly clenched.

Jordan scowled. 'If it had been that urgent then we would have flown down last night. You—'

'Leave the girl alone, Jordan,' Gideon rapped out from the front of the plane. 'Can't you see she feels ill?'

Jordan could see that all too easily. He was furious with himself for not realising how nervous Stephanie was about flying—preferably before the helicopter had taken off!

His fingers tightened about hers. 'You're an idiot for not telling me.'

'Thank you so much for that, Jordan,' Stephanie snarled back. 'Comments on my mental state are just what I want to hear when I'm hanging hundreds of feet from the ground in a helicopter that looks as if a brisk wind might blow it out of the sky!'

Gideon chuckled softly in the pilot seat. 'No need to worry, Stephanie. The accident record in this type of helicopter is minimal, I assure you.'

'Minimal, maybe,' she gritted out through her teeth. 'But not non-existent.'

'I suggest you keep any more helpful information like that to yourself, Gid,' Jordan said.

'I could always turn back—'

'No!' Stephanie shuddered at the mere thought of Gideon turning the helicopter, let alone landing it on the helipad behind Mulberry Hall.

'But if this really is a problem for you, Stephanie...?' Jordan frowned, clearly not happy.

'We're in the air now,' she said tautly, her fingers curled so tightly about Jordan's that she was sure she must be cutting off the blood supply to his own fingers. 'I'll just make a mental note to myself to never, *ever* fly in a helicopter again!'

Stephanie was grateful for having Jordan's hand to hold during the rest of the flight, but even so, by the time they landed at the private airfield a few miles outside London, where the St Claire helicopter was obviously parked when not in use, she was aching from head to toe from the pure tension of just getting through the flight. Even her teeth ached as she staggered thankfully down onto the tarmac and all but fell into the chauffeur-driven car that was waiting for them to arrive.

'All right now?' Jordan prompted gently as he climbed into the back beside her, while Gideon sat in the front with the chauffeur, the glass partition raised to give them privacy.

Stephanie dropped her head back onto the leather seat beside him, some of the colour thankfully returning to her cheeks as she swallowed before answering. 'That was the most terrifying experience of my life.'

Jordan gave a mocking grin. 'You have yet to share a house with the whole of the St Claire clan.'

Stephanie had shared a house with Jordan for the past few days, and that had been traumatic enough!

Although he looked most unlike the unkempt man she had spent those two days with. When he'd appeared in the kitchen earlier this morning his long hair had been washed and brushed back from his face in silky dark waves, his jaw freshly shaven, once again revealing that fascinating—and sexy!—dimple in the centre of his chin, and he was wearing a pale brown cashmere sweater over a cream-coloured shirt and tailored brown trousers with brown shoes.

Today he looked every inch the charismatic actor Jordan Simpson—which was probably the whole point of the exercise, when he was about to see the mother the three St Claire men so obviously all adored.

Stephanie certainly felt decidedly underdressed in the company of the handsome St Claire twins, wearing her normal jeans and a white T-shirt beneath a short black jacket. Their arrival at St Claire House in Mayfair only confirmed her rapidly growing impression—after the grandeur of the Mulberry Hall estate and then flying around in a private helicopter—that she was completely out of her depth with this family. The townhouse itself was absolutely enormous: four storeys high, with a painted cream façade.

A stiffly formal butler opened the door to admit the three of them into the cavernous entrance hall.

'Mr St Claire is in his study, and Her—*Mrs* St Claire is upstairs in her suite, resting,' the grey-haired man politely answered Jordan's query.

'I'll leave Lucan to you while I go up and see Mother,' Jordan informed Gideon, and he took a firm hold on Stephanie's elbow.

'Thanks,' his twin accepted dryly. 'No doubt I'll see you later, Stephanie.' He quirked quizzical blond brows at her.

'No doubt,' she answered distractedly.

'A tray of tea things upstairs for Miss McKinley, if you please, Parker,' Jordan instructed the butler, before putting a hand beneath Stephanie's elbow and escorting her to the back of the hallway, to open the two carved oak doors there and reveal a lift. 'My grandmother had arthritis, and had it installed fifty years ago so that she could still go upstairs,' he explained as they stepped inside the spacious mirror-walled lift.

Of course she had, Stephanie accepted ruefully; obviously the St Claire family was wealthy enough to do anything it chose.

Jordan easily read the look on her face as she stood against the opposite wall of the lift. 'Don't let all the grandeur of Mulberry Hall and here fool you—normally none of us step foot in either of these houses.'

'Why on earth not?' She frowned her curiosity.

It was a curiosity Jordan had no intention of satisfying. St Claire House, like Mulberry Hall, was part of the Duke of Stourbridge's estate, and they were all only here now because their mother, still the Duchess of Stourbridge despite the divorce, always stayed at St Claire House on the rare occasions she came down to London.

'We're all too busy doing other things,' Jordan dismissed evasively as he stepped out into the thick carpeted hallway on the third floor. 'I'll make you comfortable in my suite before I go and see my mother.'

'Your…suite?' Stephanie echoed hesitantly.

'All the family have their own suite of rooms here.' Jordan gave a brief smile at she hung back uncertainly. 'Parker will bring you tea in my private sitting room. I expect the bedroom adjoining that has been prepared for your use. Is that going to be a problem?'

Stephanie had no idea—was it? It felt a little too intimate to have him next door. Entirely too close to him for comfort, in fact!

'I would be quite happy with something a little less… grand.' She frowned her discomfort.

'There isn't anything less grand,' Jordan informed her dryly as he opened a door to the left of the hallway. 'Come on, Stephanie,' he encouraged impatiently. 'I'd like to see you settled before I go and visit my mother.'

She was being ridiculous, Stephanie knew as she followed Jordan reluctantly. It just felt so very strange to be here with him and his family, in this grand house they rarely visited, but which was still run by what was no doubt an army of servants.

Who lived like this nowadays?

Only the very rich and the titled. Although not even too many titled families managed to live in such luxury nowadays, either, years of savage inheritance taxes having depleted their ranks and fortunes drastically.

The sitting-room, decorated in subtle tones of brown

and cream, and furnished with heavy dark furniture, was very much in keeping with the luxury of the rest of this London townhouse.

'There are some books over there if you feel like reading.' Jordan indicated the shelves at the back of the room. 'My bedroom and bathroom are through there.' He pointed to a door to the right. 'And your own bedroom is through there.' He pointed to another door to the left.

Far, *far* too close for comfort, she recognised with a pained wince.

'Cheer up, Stephanie,' Jordan drawled as he saw the expression on her face. 'With any luck we can both be out of here in a matter of days.'

Days?

It was the *nights* that bothered her!

How was she supposed to sleep here when she knew that Jordan's bedroom was only feet away? Knew that the two of them were cosily ensconced in the complete privacy of his suite?

'Stop looking so worried.' Jordan leant his cane against the plush brown sofa before slowly crossing the room until he stood only inches away from her. He placed a gentle hand beneath her chin and raised her face up to his. 'I'll try to ensure this is as short a stay as possible.'

It had already been too long as far as Stephanie was concerned!

Jordan grimaced. 'Wish me luck, hmm? I'm about to put on the performance of my life,' he added ruefully.

Stephanie felt slightly breathless as she looked up searchingly into that rakishly handsome face, his close proximity having once again unnerved her. 'You want your mother to believe you're already completely recovered…' she realised slowly.

'I'm going to try to convince her of that, yes.' He shrugged. 'It'll be one less thing for her to worry about.'

'You aren't going to do anything that could hinder your progress, are you?'

Jordan sighed. 'Ever the physiotherapist, Stephanie?'

'That's probably because I *am* a physiotherapist!' she defended hotly.

Although her traitorous body certainly had other ideas. Every part of her—every muscle, sinew and nerve-ending—was totally aware of Jordan as a man rather than as a patient. Of that hand still cupping her chin. Of the warmth of Jordan's body as he stood so close to her. Of the sensuality in his warm amber-coloured gaze as it moved slowly across her slightly parted lips. The soft caress of his breath against her cheeks as his head began to lower towards hers…

Stephanie stepped back abruptly as she realised Jordan intended kissing her. 'That is definitely *not* a good idea,' she stated firmly.

Only just in time too, as a faint knock sounded on the outer door, announcing the entry of the butler with the tray of tea things Jordan had requested.

'I'll probably have lunch with my mother, but I'm sure Parker will bring you something up on a tray…' Jordan looked expectantly at the butler as he straightened from placing the silver tray down on the low table in front of the sofa.

'I would be happy to do so, Miss McKinley,' the butler replied, before Stephanie even had chance to object to being waited on in this way.

She looked across at Jordan. 'That really isn't necessary...'

'Just do it, Stephanie,' Jordan said distractedly, and he left the suite, his thoughts obviously already with his mother.

Her own thoughts were in total disarray as Parker continued to treat her as if she were a guest, rather than just another employee, informing her that her bag had been safely delivered to the adjoining bedroom.

Stephanie felt totally out of place in this world of wealth and privilege that Jordan and his brothers seemed to take so much for granted. She was even less happy at being here when she remembered that she would have to telephone Joey and tell her she was now back in London if her sister needed to talk to her about the divorce case...

CHAPTER NINE

STEPHANIE felt slightly better once she had finished drinking the pot of Earl Grey tea and eaten a couple of biscuits to settle her stomach after the helicopter flight. In fact, she felt so much better that she must have dozed off for a while, because the next thing she knew Parker had returned with her lunch tray.

But the queasiness returned with a vengeance once Stephanie had eaten the delicious pasta dish and a bowl of fresh fruit and then dared to venture into the adjoining bedroom that Jordan had said was to be hers for the duration of her stay. It was a room dominated by a huge four-poster bed draped in the same gold brocade as the chair-covers and the curtains hanging at the long picture windows, which looked out onto the meticulously kept garden at the back of the house.

It was undoubtedly a beautiful room. The gold carpet was thick and luxurious, the walls papered in a pale cream silk, the light wood furniture Regency style—and no doubt, as with Mulberry Hall, all genuine antiques. The equally luxurious *en-suite* bathroom was of cream and gold-coloured marble, with gold fixtures and several thick cream towels warming on the stand beside the slightly sunken bath.

It was all very beautiful—and totally unsuitable for someone who was, after all, just an employee.

Stephanie left her bag unpacked on one of the brocade-covered chairs and hastily backed out of that luxurious bedroom. As soon as Jordan returned from visiting his mother she would have to tell him that she couldn't stay here. That if he was really serious about wanting her professional help then she would prefer to go back to her own flat and simply visit him here every day.

In the meantime, grounding herself by chatting to Joey sounded like an excellent idea…

'Has Jordan Simpson tried to seduce you into his bed yet?' Joey questioned avidly, as soon as Stephanie's call had been put through to her office.

Not into his bed, no… 'Don't be ridiculous, Joey,' she dismissed briskly.

'And I had such high hopes, too!'

'High hopes of what?' Stephanie asked.

'Of you not continuing to live the life of a nun!'

'According to Rosalind Newman, I don't.'

'She's just a vindictive woman!' The scowl could be heard in Joey's voice.

Stephanie sighed. 'How are things going with the divorce case?'

'Nothing new, I'm afraid.' Her sister became her usual businesslike self. 'Rosalind Newman is still insisting you had an affair with her husband, and Richard Newman is doing nothing to help the situation. It could get very messy, I'm afraid, Stephs,' she added regretfully.

Exactly what Stephanie was trying to avoid. 'Perhaps if we all met up and talked about it?'

'Not a good idea,' Joey advised. 'Even if all three

lawyers were there representing their clients, it would still likely end up in a slanging match.'

On a practical level Stephanie already knew that. She just didn't know what else she could do to convince Rosalind Newman that she was being delusional about Stephanie's personal involvement with her husband. It was complicated by the fact that Stephanie was convinced Richard Newman's lack of support was because he was involved in an affair with *another* woman, and he'd rather Stephanie's name was blackened than his actual mistress's.

'Just do your best to keep my name out of it, Joey,' Stephanie said heavily.

'And you try and come up with something more interesting to tell me the next time you call,' her sister encouraged teasingly.

'By "interesting" I take it you mean sexual?' Stephanie came back dryly.

'You're with *Jordan Simpson*, sis,' Joey said impatiently. 'The man you've lusted after for years!'

The man she still lusted after, Stephanie thought. 'He isn't at all like I imagined he would be.' He was so much *more* than she had expected, she admitted privately—a man who was drawing on every ounce of strength he had to get him through the worst moments of what she knew were excruciating agony.

'In what way?' Joey prompted curiously. 'Surely you aren't holding it against him because he's behaving less like a movie star and more like a man who fell off the top of a building six months ago? Because if you are, then I hate to tell you this, Stephs, but the man *did* fall off a building six months ago!'

'No, I'm not holding that against him.' Stephanie chuckled wryly; she could always rely on Joey to make her laugh. 'Joey…' She deliberately lowered her voice. 'You know those interviews he gives, where he mentions his parents' divorce as being the reason he's never married?'

'Yes…'

'Well, he's really serious about it.' She drew in a ragged breath. 'Which means—'

'He wouldn't be too happy if he were to learn that the physiotherapist his brother hired is up to her ears in another couple's divorce?' Joey finished, with her usual bluntness.

Especially considering what they'd done together yesterday evening in his study! Stephanie thought. 'Perhaps I should try talking to Richard again?'

'No, *I'll* try,' her sister insisted. 'The man is definitely hiding something—or should I say someone?—but he seems more than happy to let you take the flak.'

Yes, Stephanie believed that too. If only the man weren't so obnoxious then maybe they could have persuaded him into telling the truth. As it was…

'Just call Richard and ask him if he will speak to *me*,' Stephanie pressed.

'Will do.' Her sister rang off with her usual abruptness.

'Care to explain who Richard is?'

Stephanie drew in her breath with a sharp hiss as she turned and saw that Jordan had come quietly back into the sitting room and now stood near the door, looking across at her with icily narrowed eyes. She stood up slowly to run her damp palms down her denim-clad thighs. 'Didn't you know that it's rude to listen to other people's telephone conversations?'

'If I did then I obviously forgot,' Jordan said unapologetically as he stepped further into the room.

The hours spent convincing his mother that he was well on the road to recovery had been just as much of a strain as Jordan had thought they might be. So much so that he was now exhausted. He had come back to his suite hoping for a rest before he had to go through the whole charade all over again at dinner. He certainly didn't appreciate coming back into his suite of rooms and overhearing the end of Stephanie's telephone conversation concerning some man called Richard that she was obviously desperate to get in touch with!

He eyed Stephanie coldly. 'Well?'

'I don't see that this has anything to do with you—'

'You told me you weren't involved with anyone,' he reminded her harshly.

'I told you I wasn't married or engaged,' she corrected. 'Which I'm not.'

'But you obviously are involved with someone. Or at least you were!'

'I— Are you okay, Jordan?' Stephanie exclaimed as she saw how pale he was.

'Do I look okay?' he snapped scathingly as he swayed slightly on his feet.

'No.' She could clearly see the grey cast to his skin, and dark shadows under his eyes, deep lines grooved beside his mouth. 'You need to take some painkillers and then lie down until they start to take effect. I'll help you into your bedroom—'

'I don't need any help!' He glared across at her.

She flinched at the vehemence in Jordan's tone. 'You obviously need to go to bed—'

'Is that an invitation, Stephanie?' he cut in. 'If it is then I think I should warn you I'm really not up to making love to you right now, and I'm not exactly in the mood, either.' Those gold eyes glittered down at her with cold satisfaction as Stephanie gave a pained gasp.

'That's enough, Jordan!'

Stephanie spun sharply round to find Lucan St Claire standing in the doorway, his austerely handsome face set in disapproving lines as he looked coldly across at his youngest brother.

The fact that the critical gaze wasn't levelled at her made absolutely no difference to Stephanie; Jordan's scornful remarks had made it more than obvious that he had made love to her before today!

Tears of mortification welled in her eyes. 'If you will both excuse me?' she choked emotionally, before hurrying into the bedroom she'd as yet had no opportunity to tell Jordan she couldn't sleep in—tonight or any other night.

'Well, that was pretty nasty even for you,' Lucan said with disapproval as he closed the door behind him before striding further into the room.

'I don't remember asking for your opinion on my behaviour, Lucan,' he muttered wearily.

His brother frowned. 'It was possible to hear your raised voice all the way down the hallway.'

His mouth twisted derisively. 'How utterly shocking!'

Lucan raised dark brows. 'Exactly what *is* your relationship with Stephanie McKinley?'

'You were the one who hired her.' Jordan turned away abruptly and began walking painfully towards his bedroom.

'That wasn't what I asked.'

'It's all you're going to get!' Jordan snapped, as each step he took caused him excruciating agony.

'Have you been to bed with her?'

Jordan came to a sudden and painful halt before slowly turning back to face his eldest brother. 'Mind your own business,' he bit out with slow precision.

'I'll take that as a yes, shall I?' Lucan murmured speculatively.

Jordan glared. 'You can take it any way you please.'

'Oh, believe me, I will,' Lucan said.

'No doubt,' Jordan muttered disgustedly.

His brother gave him an arrogant look. 'That aside, I believe you owe Miss McKinley an apology—'

'Like hell I do!'

'You deliberately set out to insult her.' Lucan gave him one of his superior looks.

Jordan knew exactly what he had done. He just wasn't sure why he had done it… What difference did it make to him whether or not Stephanie was still panting after some man called Richard she had been involved with before the two of them had even met?

His eyes narrowed. 'Tell me, Lucan—when you decided to hire her, did you do your usual check into her background?'

His brother looked unconcerned by the insult in Jordan's tone. 'Stephanie McKinley graduated top of her class—'

'I meant her *personal* background,' Jordan cut in impatiently.

'I don't believe her personal life is any of my concern. Nor,' Lucan added softly, 'if your lack of interest in her is genuine, should it be any of yours.'

No, it shouldn't, Jordan acknowledged grudgingly. Except last night had made it so…

Damn it, he had thought Stephanie was different. Had hoped that she was. And all the time she had been in his arms she had been hankering for some man called Richard.

'Unless it escaped your notice, Stephanie McKinley was crying when she ran out of here.' Lucan's mouth had thinned disapprovingly.

'I noticed,' Jordan admitted. 'But we have much more important things to worry about than Stephanie's hurt feelings, remember?'

'Let's deal with one problem at a time, hmm?' Lucan insisted. 'Your first priority is to apologise to Miss McKinley—'

'For stating the truth?'

His brother looked implacable. 'I didn't hear her calling you a cruel and heartless louse, but at the moment *that* happens to be the truth, too.'

Jordan's mouth compressed into a tight line. 'Obviously Stephanie is much more restrained than I am. Now, if you wouldn't mind, Lucan?' he added pointedly. 'I need to go and lie down before I fall down.'

He didn't wait for his brother to answer, but limped the rest of the way to his bedroom and all but slammed the door behind him before collapsing on the bed with a heartfelt sigh of relief.

Hours spent putting on an act for his mother had taken much more out of Jordan than he had expected. The conversation a few minutes ago with Stephanie even more so.

Did he owe her an apology?

Her private life was her business. A few kisses—okay, so it had been more than just a few kisses—didn't entitle Jordan to know about every man she had ever slept with.

Damn it, Lucan was right; he *did* owe Stephanie an apology!

* * *

'I'm sorry.'

Stephanie turned her head abruptly on the pillow as she looked across the room to where Jordan stood stiffly in the bedroom doorway. *Swayed* in the doorway, would actually be a better description of what he was doing. He leant heavily on his cane with one hand and held on to the doorframe with the other…

She sat up with a frown. 'You should be in bed—'

'I honestly don't think I can make it back to my own bedroom,' Jordan admitted ruefully as he staggered across the room and sank down gratefully on the side of her bed. 'I'm not sure I even have enough energy left to lie down, let alone walk.'

Stephanie was pretty sure that he didn't; his cheeks were hollow, eyes dark with pain, and his mouth was set in a grimly determined line. The same determination that had enabled him to get to her bedroom and no further…

She stood up hastily to move round to Jordan's side of the bed. 'Are you going to let me help you this time?' She was hesitant about even touching him again after the way he had reacted earlier.

He gave a pained wince. 'If you don't then I'll probably just slide onto the floor before passing out.'

Stephanie shook her head even as she took away his cane and slipped off his shoes, before helping him to lie back against the pillows and carefully swing his legs up onto the brocade bedcover. 'You shouldn't have strained yourself by even attempting to come in here.'

He glanced up at her. 'Lucan seems to think I owe you an apology.'

Stephanie stilled. 'Do *you* think you owe me an apology?'

'I was out of line earlier,' Jordan murmured honestly

as he saw the way Stephanie's gaze was avoiding meeting his.

'Yes,' she agreed flatly. 'And, as I have no intention of explaining who Richard is, I think it would better for all concerned if I went back to my own flat now, and recommended someone else to take over your therapy.'

'Lucan assures me that you're the best there is,' he said.

'Even so…'

'He also told me that your private life is none of our concern.' Those gold eyes were narrowed guardedly.

'Your brother is very—opinionated,' Stephanie acknowledged dryly.

'But he's usually right,' Jordan pointed out.

'Perhaps.' Stephanie nodded, not sure whether she was relieved or disappointed that Jordan felt the same way as Lucan. If he had continued to demand to know who Richard was, then it might have meant that he was genuinely interested in her himself. As it was, he had obviously decided, on his brother's advice, that her private life was none of his business.

A complete change of subject was necessary. 'How was your mother earlier?'

'As bright and positive as she usually is.' Jordan sighed heavily. 'The two of us put on quite a show, I can tell you—my mother pretending she's only here to shop, and me pretending that everything is going well with my recovery.'

Stephanie had yet to meet Molly St Claire, but she had no doubt that she would like her; she had to be quite something for the three formidable St Claire men to adore her in the way they obviously did. She also doubted, if Molly St Claire was as close to her sons as she appeared to be, that the other woman had been any more fooled by Jordan's act of wellbeing than he had been fooled by hers…

'You shouldn't have tried to manage without your cane,' Stephanie scolded again, as Jordan gave a low groan of pain when he tried to move his leg into a more comfortable position.

'It's never been as bad as this before,' Jordan grated, a nerve pulsing in his tightly clenched jaw. 'The muscles in my leg seem to have seized up completely.'

Stephanie no longer felt hesitant as she sat down on the side of the bed and gently ran her hands over Jordan's right leg and felt the way his muscles were locked into place. Her glance flicked up to his rigidly set face. 'Perhaps some painkillers to relax the muscles—'

'No,' he told her grimly.

Stephanie chewed on her bottom lip. 'I could probably ease some of the tension by directly massaging the muscles. But it's going to be painful,' she warned regretfully.

'Can't be any worse than it already is,' Jordan muttered through gritted teeth, his fingers curled into the brocade cover at his sides.

'It will work better if we take your trousers off…'

'Are you trying to get me naked, Stephanie?' he teased, even as he concentrated on controlling the pain.

'I believe I said your trousers, not all your clothes!' Her cheeks flushed a fiery red.

'Go ahead,' Jordan invited, and he stared rigidly up at the canopy overhead, knowing that the depth of his pain was his own fault after trying to manage without his cane for a couple of hours. 'I'm certainly in no condition to stop you,' he added slightly bitterly.

Stephanie tried hard to maintain a professional façade as she unbuttoned and unzipped Jordan's trousers, before sliding them down his thighs to reveal the figure-hugging black boxers he wore beneath. Inwardly it was a different matter, however, as her fingers brushed lightly over his muscled abdomen and legs before she removed the trousers altogether and forced her gaze down to look at his legs.

His left leg was lean and muscled, covered in a dusting of dark hair and slightly tanned, but his right leg showed the white scars from the operations he had undergone these last six months, with the muscles in his thigh visibly knotted beneath the tautly stretched skin.

Stephanie winced inwardly at the thought of the pain Jordan would experience when she attempted to massage those locked muscles without the help of painkillers.

'Perhaps you should drink a couple of glasses of wine before I start—'

'Just do it, Stephanie,' Jordan encouraged gruffly, obviously guessing the reason for her hesitation.

She drew in a controlling breath as she firmly reminded herself that she was a professional. That she had to forget she had been intimate with this man and just do the job Lucan St Claire had asked her to do.

Jordan closed his eyes and clenched his teeth tightly together as he felt the first touch of Stephanie's fingers against the rigid hardness of his thigh. Keeping his eyes closed and teeth tightly clenched, he concentrated on not crying out as she began to massage and work those tense muscles. Over and over again. Until Jordan finally began to feel a slight lessening of that tension, and the rest of his body also began to relax as the pain began to ease.

'Magic,' he murmured huskily minutes later, as he finally found he could ease back onto the bedcovers.

'Training,' Stephanie dismissed briskly.

Now that the pain was easing slightly Jordan had a chance to look up at Stephanie as she continued to massage his thigh. To note how her cheeks had become flushed by her exertions. How the tip of her tongue was caught between her teeth as she concentrated. How several wisps of her fiery hair had come loose from her plait to fall unnoticed against those flushed cheeks.

'I think you can stop now.'

Stephanie gave Jordan a startled glance, having been concentrating so intensely on easing his pain that she hadn't noticed that the pain had obviously stopped and his attention had now shifted to her…

She stopped massaging his thigh to sit back abruptly. 'You should be able to sleep now.'

'I intend to,' Jordan said. 'Join me?' He held out his hand in invitation.

An invitation that Stephanie didn't take. Instead she looked down at him warily.

Jordan knew that his behaviour earlier had been completely out of line. That things had happened between the two of them so fast at Mulberry Hall, so intensely, there had been no real opportunity for either of them to talk about past or present relationships.

Maybe Stephanie *did* still have a thing for some guy she had known in the past—but it hadn't stopped her from responding to him, had it?

'Please?' he invited huskily.

Stephanie had no idea what Jordan had been thinking about during the last few minutes' silence, but after their earlier conversation it didn't take a great deal of imagination on her part to guess what it might have been!

Or for her to know that Jordan had completely the wrong idea about her relationship with Richard Newman. She wanted to tell him, but she knew that the truth would be even less acceptable to him.

'I promise I'll be good,' Jordan added cajolingly.

Stephanie gave a little laugh. 'Does this little-boy-lost act usually work?'

'On doting mothers and dedicated physiotherapists? Hopefully, yes!'

She gave a rueful shake of her head. 'You're impossible.'

'But endearing?' He held his hand out to her once again.

After the briefest of pauses Stephanie put her hand into his and allowed him to pull her down beside him on the bed, shifting slightly onto his side as he took her into his arms.

A few minutes of heaven couldn't hurt, could it? Stephanie promised herself.

Just a few minutes.

CHAPTER TEN

IT WAS already starting to get dark outside when Jordan woke up from the most refreshing sleep he'd had for months, with the still sleeping Stephanie held tightly in his arms.

Her hair had once again come loose from that confining plait, and now lay in a silky curtain of fire and gold across his chest and shoulder. Her lashes were long and dark against her creamy cheeks, and that smattering of freckles on the bridge of her nose totally enticing. Her lips were slightly parted as she breathed softly.

Jordan could feel the warmth of her hand as it lay against his chest, and the heat of her leg as it lay lightly entangled with his. A heat that seeped deep into Jordan's own body as he felt himself becoming aroused by Stephanie's proximity.

He turned carefully onto his side in an effort not to wake her, knowing that if Stephanie were awake she would probably insist that nothing of a personal nature be allowed to happen between them.

Such as Jordan running his hand slowly down her spine. Such as allowing that hand to trace her waist and hip. Such as cupping her bottom as he fitted the length of her body perfectly against his. Such as placing his mouth against her brow and temple before exploring the soft curve of her warm cheek in a direct path to the lips he longed to claim with his own…

Stephanie was sure she had to be still dreaming when she woke in the semi-darkness and found herself pressed against a hard male body. She felt warm and sure hands moving over her in exploration, the hot caress of lips against her brow, temple, cheek, and—

As Jordan's lips claimed hers Stephanie knew this was no dream. She really was lying on a bed with the semi-naked Jordan St Claire!

She pulled her mouth away from his even as her hand pushed against the hard chest pressed so firmly against her breasts. 'No, Jordan!'

'Oh, yes, Stephanie,' he murmured throatily, and he continued to hold her against him, with his hands pressed against her bottom, his lips now moving down the length of her neck and throat.

She had known sleeping with Jordan was a bad idea from the start. It was the reason she had fought so strongly against it. Because she had no defences against this man. The feelings she'd realised she had for him had stripped away all those defences and left only raw, unadulterated passion in their place.

'God, you taste good!' Jordan groaned as his lips returned to claim hers.

He tasted better than good. He was earth, and spice, and irresistible heat…

He parted the lips beneath his as he felt Stephanie curve her body into his, her hands moving up his chest and her fingers becoming entangled in his hair.

They kissed heatedly, hungrily. Lips, teeth and tongues exploring, biting, possessing, as their hunger for each other spiralled wildly, became mindless, out of all control.

It wasn't enough. Jordan wanted more.

'I need to see you—to touch you!'

Jordan quickly removed her jeans and panties before taking off her T-shirt to bare those perfect breasts, drinking his fill of her slender nakedness. Then he slowly lowered his head to claim one of those turgid nipples into the heat of his mouth, to stroking it with his tongue as his hand caressed a path down to those silky curls between her thighs.

Stephanie was beyond thought, beyond anything but the perfection of Jordan's lovemaking. Her back arched to press her breast into the heat of his mouth even as her thighs moved rhythmically against the caress of his fingers.

It wasn't enough. Stephanie wanted more.

She pulled away to sit up and roll Jordan's T-shirt up, before pulling it completely over his head to bare his torso to the exploration of her avid lips and tongue.

Kissing his heated flesh, licking him, she moved down the length of his chest to his navel, pausing there to dip her tongue into that shallow well, the heat between her own thighs intensifying as she heard Jordan's groan of pleasure.

She knelt beside him, able to see the length of his arousal pressing urgently against his boxers, and her fingers reached up for the waistband to roll them down his thighs and legs and remove them completely. Releasing the hard jut of his arousal to her heated gaze.

He was beautiful, so long and thick, and Stephanie moved to kneel between Jordan's parted legs and curled her fingers about that pulsing velvet-soft flesh, her other hand cupping him beneath.

'Dear God!' Jordan's back arched at the first lick of her hot little tongue against his engorged flesh, and he tightened the fingers of both hands in the bedcover beneath him as she slowly ran the tip of her tongue along the firm length of him, from base to tip, lingering to swirl around the sensitive head even as her hands continued to caress the length of him.

Over and over again she caressed and licked and swirled, building the tension inside Jordan to an unbearable degree. But not so unbearable that he wanted her to stop!

'Stephanie…' He gave an aching groan as she finally claimed him in her hot mouth, driving Jordan to the point of insanity. Much more of this and he knew he was going to lose control completely!

Stephanie looked slightly dazed as Jordan sat up to place his hands on her shoulders before gently pushing her away from him.

'Don't look at me like that,' he murmured, as he manoeuvred her over him, so that her knees were placed either side of his thighs. He lay back on the bed, his arousal against the moist, hot core of her. 'I want to be inside you, Stephanie,' he pleaded throatily. 'Deep inside you.' His gaze held hers as he entered her, inch by slow, pleasurable inch.

Stephanie gasped as she felt herself stretching, accommodating his size. Her flesh was pulsing as she reached down to balance herself above him with her hands on his shoulders, as she lowered down onto the width and length of him until she sheathed him completely from tip to hilt.

'That is so good…' Jordan's eyes glowed golden in the darkness as he reached out to place his hands on her hips. 'But I'm afraid you're going to have to do all the hard work now, Stephanie.'

Her cheeks were flushed, her breathing ragged as

she began to move, slowly at first, and then harder and faster. Jordan's hands cupped her breasts to capture the nipples between thumb and finger. He rolled and squeezed them, increasing those pulses of pleasure deep between her thighs to an almost unbearable degree.

She moved harder and faster still, and she felt Jordan become even harder inside her as he approached his own release. She gasped breathlessly as he moved one of his hands and his fingers found and stroked that swollen nubbin nestled in her curls, tipping her over the edge of release. At the same moment she heard him cry out, continuing to ride him as long as his hot, pulsing pleasure consumed them both.

Finally Stephanie collapsed weakly against Jordan's chest, her pulse still racing, her breathing ragged. Jordan's arms came about her and she felt him gently smoothing the fiery strands of her unconfined hair down her back. 'Thank you.'

Stephanie looked at him quizzically as she raised her head. 'Shouldn't I be the one saying that?'

He smiled. 'Surely the pleasure was mutual?'

The pleasure… Oh, God, the pleasure! Stephanie had never known anything like it before. Those few exploratory forays she had made into the physical side of sex while at university didn't even begin to compare to making love with Jordan. To the wonder of having him inside her still.

Except this should never have happened.

She was the physiotherapist Lucan St Claire had employed with the expectation that she would help Jordan regain the full mobility of his damaged leg; he certainly hadn't employed her to go to bed with his brother!

And she really *had* been to bed with him now. Had slept with him. Made love with him.

'Stop that!' Jordan instructed harshly as he saw and guessed the reason for Stephanie's suddenly pained expression.

'I can't,' she groaned.

'Stephanie—'

'I need to go to the bathroom.' Her gaze avoided his as she moved carefully upwards to release him before shifting to the side of the bed to stand up and collect her clothes from the floor. She held them in front of her protectively. 'I think it would be—be better for both of us if you've gone back to your own bedroom by the time I return.'

She could have no idea how absolutely beautiful she looked, standing there with nothing but a few scraps of clothing held in front of her to hide her nakedness. Her hair was a red-gold tangle about the slenderness of her shoulders, her eyes sultry from her release, and her lips were still swollen from the heat of the kisses they had shared.

Even so, Jordan knew from her behaviour that she regretted what had just happened between the two of them. Because of this Richard guy?

He sat up on the side of the bed, feeling only a twinge of discomfort in his leg as he did so. 'We need to talk about this, Stephanie—'

'There is no *"this"*!' Her eyes flashed deeply green. 'It shouldn't have happened, Jordan.' She held her clothes even more tightly against her.

He grimaced. 'I believe your next line is, *This was a mistake*.'

'It *was* a mistake!' She glared at him.

Jordan sighed. 'Look, I realise that you're upset—'

'Upset?' Stephanie echoed. 'I'm devastated!'

'We can talk this out—'

'No, we can't,' she said. 'I can't stay here. I have to leave. I'm sorry I won't be able to help you after all, but—'

'You *have* helped me, Stephanie,' he said gruffly. 'In ways you can't even begin to imagine.'

She became very still. 'By going to bed with you?'

He winced. 'As it happens, yes.'

She took a step back, even as she looked at him searchingly. The sudden glitter that appeared in those deep green eyes said she didn't like what she saw! 'You've had doubts since the accident about your ability to make love to a woman,' she realised incredulously.

Jordan scowled. 'I wouldn't put it quite like that—'

'I would!' She gritted her teeth. 'Well, aren't I the lucky one? I had no idea I was helping to restore the sexual confidence of the legendary lover Jordan Simpson!'

'Damn it, it was interest that I lacked—not sexual confidence!'

Obviously he hadn't expected to feel like making love to anyone immediately after the accident; he had been in so much pain at the time there hadn't been room for him to feel anything else. But once he had recovered enough to be discharged from hospital, to have friends come over to his house in Malibu, Jordan had thought he might resume his relationship with Crista. After only a few minutes spent in her company, though, he had known that he no longer wanted her. In his life or in his bed.

As the days and weeks had passed, Jordan had realised that he didn't want *any* of the beautiful women—models and actress friends—who'd come to his house and blatantly let him know they would be only too happy to fill the place Crista had once had in his life.

He hadn't wanted any of them.

Until Stephanie.

Stephanie McKinley had burst into his life like a refreshing breeze. Answering him back. Challenging him. Arousing him…

She gave an impatient shake of her head now. 'Well, I'm sure you'll be glad to know you haven't lost your touch in the slightest! Now, if you will excuse me—'

'No, I *won't* excuse you!' Jordan surged to his feet and reached out to grasp her arm and turn her forcibly back to face him. 'You're twisting this conversation deliberately because of your relationship with someone called Richard—'

'I do *not* have a relationship with someone called Richard!'

'Not any more, no,' Jordan accepted. 'I thought that was the problem,' he said. 'But don't you see that the fact you respond to *me* shows your feelings for this other guy aren't as strong as you think they are? That you wouldn't have been able to respond in the way you did just now if you were in love with someone else?'

She looked mutinous. 'I refuse to talk about this any more, Jordan.'

Jordan frowned down at her, frustrated. Half of him wanted to kiss her again, and the other half wanted to tan her obstinate little bottom. Either solution was guaranteed to make Stephanie even angrier in her present mood. 'Maybe we can talk again once you've had time to calm down?' he suggested through gritted teeth.

Those green eyes flashed in warning before she wrenched out of his grasp. 'I very much doubt that I'm going to calm down any time soon,' she said scathingly. 'Now, please *leave*!' She marched into the adjoining bathroom and slammed the door loudly behind her.

Having given Jordan a tantalising glimpse of her bare and perfectly shaped bottom!

Not his finest hour, he recognised with a pained grimace as he heard the shower being turned on as another way of Stephanie telling him she had no intention of coming out of the bathroom until after he had left.

His movements were slow as he pulled his clothes back on before using his cane to stand up and glare at that closed bathroom door. Stephanie might not want to talk to him, but she was damn well going to listen to what he had to say. And soon!

He came to an abrupt halt when he entered the adjoining sitting room to find Gideon relaxing on the sofa, idly flicking through a magazine. 'How long have you been in here?' His eyes were narrowed suspiciously.

Gideon looked across at him mockingly as he put the magazine down before standing up. 'Legendary lover?' he drawled speculatively.

'Oh, go to hell, Gid!' Jordan limped across the room into his bedroom, slamming the door just as loudly behind him as Stephanie had the bathroom door a few minutes ago.

And just as finally…

It took Stephanie only ten minutes or so to shower and dress in the bathroom, deliberately keeping her gaze firmly averted from the rumpled covers on the four-poster bed when she came back into the bedroom to collect her coat and bag.

She hurried out of the bedroom as if the devil were snapping at her heels. Or those erotic memories of herself and Jordan naked on the bed as they made love together!

'Leaving us so soon, Stephanie…?'

She turned sharply from closing the bedroom door to find Gideon St Claire leaning casually against the wall just outside the door to Jordan's suite.

Her chin rose defensively as she saw the dark speculation in Gideon's eyes. 'Obviously, with your mother here, you're all going to be kept pretty busy over the next few days, so I thought I might as well go back to my own flat.'

He gave her a straight look. 'I totally agree. Jordan can be a complete and utter ass.'

Stephanie felt warm colour bloom in her cheeks and cursed her fair skin—not for the first time. 'I don't believe I mentioned Jordan…'

'But you were thinking it,' Gideon said knowingly as he straightened. 'My mother would like to meet you.'

Stephanie's chest clenched in panic at the thought of being introduced to the matriarch of the St Claire family when she had so recently made love with her youngest son. 'I don't think that's a good idea.'

'Why not?'

'Well— Because—' She straightened her shoulders and looked him in the eye. 'I won't be coming back here again after today, Gideon.'

Blond brows rose. 'And that precludes you being introduced to my mother?'

'It makes it…an unnecessary complication.' Stephanie gave him a look, pleading with him to understand what she wasn't saying.

Gideon gave a grim smile. 'Can things between you and Jordan get any more complicated?'

Stephanie felt the colour draining from her cheeks as rapidly as it had entered. This man knew exactly what had happened in Stephanie's bedroom a short time ago.

'Obviously not.' She could no longer meet that knowing dark gaze.

'So you're just going to run away? Is that it?' Gideon asked.

Stephanie's mouth firmed. 'Lucan employed me as a physiotherapist for Jordan. Obviously that is no longer possible. There's nothing more I can do here,' she added determinedly as Gideon continued to look at her from between narrowed lids.

His mouth thinned. 'You've already done more for Jordan than anyone else has been able to do since the accident.'

'So I understand,' she said self-consciously.

Gideon gave a rueful smile. 'Actually, I wasn't referring to any personal relationship the two of you might or might not have.'

'Contrary to what you may have thought or assumed, I don't *have* a personal relationship with your brother,' Stephanie told him determinedly. 'I really do have to go now—' She broke off as Gideon reached out and lightly clasped her arm.

'Before you went to Gloucestershire Jordan had shut himself off from everyone. Had become completely reclusive. Uncommunicative.' He shook his head grimly as he slowly released her. 'It had gone on for so long that we had all begun to think he was never going to come out of it. He changed after you went there, Stephanie.' His expression softened. 'I could see the difference in him immediately after I arrived at Mulberry Hall yesterday.'

'I didn't do *anything*—'

'You didn't need to do anything but be yourself,' Gideon assured her. 'Watching the two of you together,

I've realised that it's the very nature of your personality which provokes him. Challenges him.'

'I'm not sure that saying I get on Jordan's nerves enough to provoke him into doing things is altogether flattering—'

'You're deliberately misunderstanding me,' Gideon said shrewdly.

'No, Gideon, I'm not.' She sighed, then reached out and gave his arm an apologetic squeeze, knowing that his concern for his twin was genuine. 'I'm pleased if you think I've annoyed Jordan enough that it's challenged him out of his seclusion at last, but my decision to leave is based solely on my own needs—not his. I simply can't stay on here any longer after— Well, I just can't,' she said emotionally.

'Do you think Jordan is just going to let you walk out of his life?'

Her eyes widened. 'Don't you?'

He gave her a wicked smile—the exact twin of Jordan's. 'Knowing Jordan, I somehow doubt it.'

Stephanie locked suddenly weak knees. 'I'm sure you're wrong.'

At least she hoped Gideon was wrong.

There was absolutely no future for herself and Jordan that Stephanie could see. Even if she could persuade him into believing she wasn't involved in a relationship with Richard Newman, he was still a world-famous actor while she was a mere physiotherapist. Jordan lived and worked in America; she lived and worked in England. This house, the private helicopter, the opulence of the Mulberry Hall estate—all of those things were an indication of the gulf there was between them, both socially and financially.

And, worst of all, Stephanie knew she had been

nothing more than a diversion for Jordan. A pique to his interest. Once he was back to his full health, back in LA and working again, he would forget that Stephanie McKinley even existed!

CHAPTER ELEVEN

'WHAT are you doing here, Jordan?'

Jordan scowled as Stephanie showed all too clearly, by the way she'd deliberately kept the door to her flat half-closed, that she had no intention of inviting him inside. 'Surely it's obvious why I'm here?' he bit out impatiently as he leant heavily on his cane.

He had spent the morning at the clinic with his mother, and now his hip and leg were aching from that and from the sheer effort of getting to Stephanie's apartment building—let alone discovering there was no lift when he got here, and so having to walk up two flights of stairs to her flat on the second floor.

'Not to me.' She gave a shake of her head.

Her hair was pulled back in a ponytail today, and she was dressed in a figure-hugging blue T-shirt and faded low-slung jeans. But her make-up-less face was so pale that the sprinkling of freckles across her nose showed in stark relief.

'I suggest you invite me inside, Stephanie, before you end up with an unconscious man on your doorstep,' Jordan warned her suddenly.

Stephanie kept the door half-closed as she looked at Jordan searchingly, noting the strain beside his eyes and mouth, and the slight pallor of his cheeks beneath his tan. 'How did your mother's appointment with the specialist go this morning?' She was concerned for the other woman, in spite of knowing that she wouldn't be having anything further to do with any of the St Claire family members.

Jordan had made it more than obvious from his remarks yesterday that what had happened between the two of them had meant nothing more to him than a reaffirmation of physical desire.

Just as Stephanie knew it had meant everything to her.

She had long been infatuated by Jordan Simpson. In lust with him, even, as she'd gazed at him wistfully on the big and small screen. But in the past few days she had fallen completely in love with Jordan St Claire. Quite how it had happened Stephanie had no idea, when he had been either rude or inappropriately over-familiar since the moment they'd first met. She only knew that she was in love with the man she had made love with yesterday. Totally. Irrevocably.

Unfortunately, the wealthy and privileged Jordan St Claire was as unlikely to fall in love with someone like her as Jordan Simpson was…

'Jord—' She broke off with a nervy start as the telephone began to ring in her flat.

The disturbing hang-up calls that had been part of Stephanie's reason for wanting to leave London had resumed first thing this morning. Four so far. Stephanie had answered the first two, only to have the line abruptly disconnected.

It wasn't difficult to know who was making those calls, and Stephanie had called Joey and asked her to use her legal influence with the telephone company and get her a new number as soon as possible.

Too late, Stephanie realised she should have taken the receiver off the hook while she was waiting for that new number!

Jordan quirked dark brows. 'Aren't you going to answer that?'

Stephanie gave a tense shrug. 'They'll call back if it's anything important.'

'If you let me in and answer the call then they won't need to call back,' he reasoned lightly.

Stephanie frowned her irritation. 'We have nothing to say to each other, Jordan—'

'You may not have anything to say to me,' he accepted grimly, 'but I certainly have a few things I want to say to you.' He didn't wait for Stephanie to open the door further, but instead pushed against it with his cane and walked into the flat, leaving her to close the door behind him.

At least the telephone had stopped ringing by the time she'd followed Jordan through to her sitting room. 'Well?' Stephanie prompted guardedly as she watched him drop down wearily into one of the armchairs.

His hair was as wild and windblown as ever, but he had shaved at least, and was wearing a tailored black jacket over a white shirt and faded jeans.

Jordan didn't answer her immediately, but instead looked around the sitting room. He liked the simplicity of the warm cream walls, adorned with several Turner prints of Venice. There were three colourful rugs on the polished wood floor, and the only furniture was a wide-screen television set, a low coffee table, a comfortable terracotta-coloured sofa, and two armchairs covered in numerous cushions. Despite the simplicity of the décor, Jordan found the room as warm and inviting as Stephanie was herself.

Although Jordan had to admit she didn't look very inviting at the moment, as she glared down at him!

He answered her earlier question evenly. 'Tests showed my mother's tumour to be benign.'

'That must be a relief for all of you!' Stephanie spoke with her first genuine warmth since she had opened the knock on the door and found Jordan standing outside.

'Yes.' He nodded tersely, eyes narrowed. 'Stephanie, why did you leave without saying goodbye?'

She clasped her hands tightly together so that he shouldn't see how they were shaking. 'I did what I thought was best.'

'For whom?'

'For me, actually,' she said honestly. 'For you too, of course. It would just have been awkward for everyone if I had stayed on at St Claire House after what happened between us yesterday.'

Jordan raised dark brows. 'I don't embarrass that easily.'

'Lucky you,' Stephanie said. 'When I went downstairs Lucan came out of his study to tell me my car had been delivered from Gloucestershire. I explained to him then that I didn't feel I could do anything to help you. He seemed happy with my decision to leave,' she said firmly.

'*I'm* not happy with your decision!' Jordan barked.

Her chin rose defensively. 'No? Well. You're probably just a little…irritated with me at the moment. But you'll get over it.'

'I'm upset, Stephanie, not irritated!' he corrected. 'We need to talk, and you left before we had a chance to do that.' He sat forward tensely.

'Because I have nothing else to say to you—' Stephanie broke off as the telephone began to ring again. She should definitely have taken the receiver off the hook. And she would have done so if she hadn't been waiting for the telephone company to ring her and tell her about her new number. It might even be them ringing now. But with Jordan present Stephanie didn't feel inclined to answer the call only to discover that it was Rosalind Newman making a nuisance of herself again.

Stephanie felt for the other woman, she really did, but that didn't make it any easier for her to be the fixation of the other woman's obsessive jealousy.

Jordan eyed her impatiently as she ignored the call. 'If you won't answer that, then I will!' He reached out for the receiver.

'No—' Stephanie gave up her effort to prevent him from answering the call as Jordan placed the receiver to his ear.

'Stephanie McKinley's residence.' Jordan spoke pleasantly into the receiver as he eyed Stephanie mockingly. 'Hello?' He frowned. 'Hello!' he repeated sharply, a dark frown now marring his brow. 'What the hell—?' He held the receiver away from his ear before slowly replacing it on the cradle and turning back to Stephanie, brows raised questioningly.

She moistened dry lips, knowing from Jordan's expression that this fifth call had to have ended as abruptly as the previous four. 'I—I seem to have a crank caller at the moment,' she dismissed, her gaze not quite meeting Jordan's probing one. 'The telephone company has been informed, and they're organising a new number for me.'

'Why not the police? And how long is "at the moment"?' Jordan asked slowly.

'The police are far too busy for me to worry them

about some idiot making a nuisance of themselves on the telephone,' Stephanie said hurriedly. 'It's been happening for a couple of weeks now. It's just been especially annoying this morning.' Probably because she hadn't been there to answer the calls for the past three days!

'A couple of weeks or so?' Jordan repeated incredulously as he stood up. 'Some nut has been harassing you like this for weeks, and you've only now decided to do anything about it? Your sister is a lawyer—why didn't you get her to do something about them before now?'

Because Stephanie hadn't mentioned the calls to Joey originally—had been stupid enough to hope that Rosalind would stop before either the law or the police needed to be involved!

'She's doing something about it now.'

'Not soon enough, by the state of your nerves!'

Stephanie moved away restlessly. 'They're just hang-up calls, Jordan. She— They'll get tired of it eventually and stop.'

'She?' Jordan pounced shrewdly.

'He. She.' Stephanie frowned her exasperation with his astuteness in picking up on every word she said. 'What does it matter what sex they are?'

'It doesn't,' Jordan said. 'Unless you *know* who's making the calls?'

'And why do you suppose I would know that?'

'You tell me,' Jordan said.

He had been absolutely furious last night, when he'd discovered that Stephanie had left St Claire House without so much as telling him. So furious that he had decided it would be better to delay coming here to see her until today, giving a chance for that anger to subside overnight. A few minutes in her company and he knew that twelve hours' delay had been a complete waste of his time!

'Stephanie!' he prompted harshly.

She clasped her hands even more tightly together as she scowled at him. 'It's none of your business, Jordan.'

'I'm making it my business,' he said.

Stephanie shook her head. 'You don't have the right to come here and demand to know about my private life.'

'By taking my body into yours you've given me that right,' he said outrageously.

Colour warmed her cheeks and she gasped. 'That was completely uncalled for, Jordan!'

Jordan threw his cane down on the sofa to reach out and grasp the tops of her arms. 'As your leaving yesterday without saying goodbye to me was completely uncalled for!' He glowered down at her. 'How do you think that made me feel, Stephanie?' His voice gentled. 'I know that you were upset last night, but that still doesn't excuse just walking out on me like that without any explanation.'

'The fact that I did leave should have been explanation enough,' she said exasperatedly.

Jordan released her, to take a halting step backwards, his face pale. 'It was your way of telling me you would prefer that our relationship not continue?'

'We don't *have* a relationship, Jordan,' Stephanie said emotionally. 'You said from the beginning that you were only playing with me—'

'What's your excuse?' he rasped harshly. 'Is it still this guy Richard?'

'I've told you that it isn't!' she insisted vehemently.

'Then what is it?'

'You're Jordan Simpson!' she snapped.

He eyed her warily. 'So?'

'So I've had a thing about you for *years*!'

'A thing?' Jordan repeated softly.

'A thing,' Stephanie repeated uncomfortably. 'Look at my DVD collection, Jordan.' She pointed to the cabinet next to the wide-screen television set. 'I have bought every film you've ever made. But not before I dragged my sister to the cinema to see every one of them first. My idea of an enjoyable evening at home is to put on one of your movies and sit and drool over you for a couple of hours!'

A nerve pulsed in Jordan's tightly clenched jaw. 'So this *thing* you have is only for Jordan Simpson?'

No, of course it wasn't! Stephanie's infatuation, maybe. But it was Jordan St Claire she had fallen in love with. A man as unlike the suavely charming and sophisticated screen image of Jordan Simpson as it was possible to for him to be...

Something Stephanie had no intention of ever admitting, least of all to Jordan himself!

'Yes,' she confirmed flatly. 'I'm sorry, Jordan.' She winced as she saw the way his expression had darkened ominously. 'I just—I did try not to get personally involved with you. I told you that it wasn't a good idea. But you've always been this fantasy to me, you see, and so when I found myself in bed with you yesterday—'

'You don't need to say any more,' he rasped harshly, those gold-coloured eyes as hard as the metal they resembled. He looked absolutely livid. 'I somehow never imagined you as a movie-star groupie—'

'I wouldn't go that far,' she cut in indignantly.

'I would,' he bit out frigidly. 'A pity for you that we've met when I'm obviously looking and feeling less than my best,' he added contemptuously as he bent to pick up his cane. 'I obviously didn't come even close to living up to the fantasy!'

Stephanie hated this conversation. *Hated* it!

She loved this man. Not Jordan Simpson. Not even Jordan St Claire. But the man standing in front of her right now. The man who in Gloucestershire had still been able to tease despite the fact that he was in constant pain. The man who had made love with her yesterday with a fierce heat she was never going to be able to forget. That she never wanted to forget. Just as she knew she never wanted to forget Jordan…

She wished things could be different. Wished that she could explain about Richard Newman to Jordan—that she could tell him the truth and that he would tell her he believed her. That he loved her too. But Jordan didn't love her, and he never would. After all, he had only made love with her to prove he could still desire a woman that way.

Which left Stephanie with no alternative but to try and salvage as much of her pride as she could. 'I don't have any complaints.' She shrugged.

Jordan's mouth compressed as he looked at her challengingly. 'Neither do I.'

Stephanie felt the warmth of colour in her cheeks. 'Then—' She broke off with a frown as the doorbell rang. 'That could be someone from the telephone company.'

'I don't think they usually make house-calls in order to change a number,' Jordan said.

Neither did Stephanie. Which was why she was reluctant to actually go and open the door…

Jordan found he was even more angry now than he had been the previous evening! Angry and disappointed that Stephanie was obviously as enamoured of his screen image as so many of the other women he'd met, rather than being attracted to the man he actually was.

He had dreamed of becoming a professional actor from the time he'd starred in a school play at the age of eleven. Had chosen to go to drama school rather than university. Done several years of stage work in England before being offered a film role in America ten years ago.

He enjoyed the success he had made of his career. Enjoyed the lifestyle it gave him. The celebrity status. But one of the drawbacks had always been that women were attracted to Jordan Simpson rather than Jordan St Claire, and unfortunately Stephanie was no exception…

He sighed heavily. 'It's time I was leaving—' He frowned as the doorbell rang again—longer this time, and somehow more insistent. 'Shouldn't you go and see who that is?' he asked, as Stephanie continued to ignore this second, much longer ring of the doorbell.

'I thought you said it was important that we finish our conversation?'

Jordan studied her through narrowed lids, once again noting that pallor to her cheeks and the wariness of her gaze. 'As far as I'm aware, it's finished.'

She gave him a bright, meaningless smile. 'I'm not in the mood for more visitors this morning.'

Jordan scowled at her obvious reluctance to answer the door. 'Stephanie, what the hell is going on here?'

'Nothing,' she denied hastily.

His scowl deepened. 'I don't believe you.'

Her eyes widened. 'I don't have to explain myself to you—'

'You're right, you don't,' Jordan said as he turned

to walk haltingly towards the door of the flat. 'Maybe your visitor will be a little more forthcoming?'

'No, Jordan—'

Jordan had wrenched the door open before Stephanie had fully realised his intention, frowning as he looked at the woman who stood outside in the hallway.

From Stephanie's evasive behaviour he had expected that her visitor would be a man. Perhaps this Richard he'd wanted to know about...

But the woman standing in the hallway was tall and blonde, probably aged in her mid-thirties, and the angry glitter of her blue eyes as she looked past Jordan to glare at Stephanie seemed to indicate that she was feeling less than friendly towards her!

Those blue eyes flicked scornfully over Jordan, before moving down to his cane. 'Another one, Stephanie?' the woman said insultingly.

'I—'

'Another what?' Jordan asked in a steely voice.

'Perhaps you aren't aware of it, but Stephanie makes a habit of having affairs with her patients,' the woman said. 'First my husband, and now you!'

This had to be Stephanie's worst nightmare!

Having Rosalind Newman arrive on her doorstep at all was bad enough, but having her make these awful accusations in front of Jordan was even worse.

She took a step forward. 'Rosalind, you aren't well—'

'I'm perfectly well, thank you!' the older woman snapped contemptuously.

The last few months of the emotional turmoil of her disintegrating marriage had not been kind to Rosalind; she was much too thin, and her face was much harder, older, than when Stephanie had first met her three months ago.

'Or as well as I can be after you stole my husband from me!' Rosalind spat out. 'Does Richard know about *him*?' She glared at Jordan.

Stephanie couldn't even look at Jordan to see what he was making of this conversation. She stepped around him so that she could confront Rosalind. Although he could hardly have been left in any doubt as to exactly what Rosalind was accusing her of! 'There's nothing to know, Rosalind,' she said soothingly. 'And even if there was it would be none of Richard's business. For the last time—I'm not and I never have been involved in an affair with your husband. He was my patient, yes, but that was the extent of our relationship.'

Blue eyes narrowed viciously. 'I don't believe you.'

'I know you don't.' Stephanie sighed heavily. 'And I'm really sorry that you don't. But that doesn't make it any less the truth.'

Rosalind raised her hands, her fingers curled like talons about to strike. 'You're nothing but a marriage-wrecking little—'

'I think not!' Jordan raised his cane to fend off the attack of those fingers as the woman would have reached out and raked her nails down Stephanie's face. 'Go home,' he told the other woman firmly as he stepped protectively in front of an obviously shaken Stephanie.

'I haven't finished yet—'

'Oh, yes, you have,' Jordan said. 'And if you want to know who wrecked your marriage then I suggest you try looking in a mirror,' he added bluntly.

'How dare you—?' The woman broke off abruptly as she seemed to look at him for the first time. 'Do I know you?'

'No, thank God!' Jordan said with feeling.

'You look very familiar...'

Jordan's mouth quirked. 'I get that all the time.'

The woman blinked dazedly. 'Are the two of you... involved?'

Jordan didn't even hesitate. 'Yes.'

'I—I don't understand.' She looked far less sure of herself now. 'What about Richard?' She looked frowningly at Stephanie.

'Stephanie has already told you that she isn't and never has been involved with your husband,' Jordan reiterated.

'I— But I'm divorcing him because of her!'

'I'm sorry about that.' Jordan frowned. 'But you've made a mistake concerning her involvement. Now, if you wouldn't mind...?' He carefully eased the woman back with his cane until she was once again fully outside in the hallway. 'I advise you not to come here and bother Stephanie again,' he said.

Anger seemed to have given way to confusion, as if the woman wasn't even sure how she came to be here now.

'I think you need to get some professional help before you end up actually hurting someone other than yourself,' Jordan added gently.

'I... Yes.' The woman turned away.

'Rosalind—'

'Let her go, Stephanie!' Jordan instructed swiftly as she made a move as if to follow the other woman. 'Leave her with some pride, damn it!'

Stephanie came to an abrupt halt, her breath catching in her throat as she looked up at Jordan and saw the expression in those beautiful gold-coloured eyes.

Despite his defence of her just now, both verbally

and physically, Jordan was obviously still far from convinced of her innocence in the breakdown of Rosalind Newman's marriage…

CHAPTER TWELVE

'Is SHE also the one making the telephone calls?'

Stephanie had staggered back into her flat to walk through to the kitchen and automatically go through the motions of making a pot of coffee. Certain, as she heard her flat door being closed seconds later, that Jordan had taken the opportunity to leave. Obviously she had been wrong…

She turned to face him across her red and white kitchen as he stood in the doorway, leaning heavily on his cane, the expression in those gold-coloured eyes hidden by narrowed lids. 'Yes,' she admitted wearily.

Jordan nodded. 'And having a man answer the last call was reason enough for her to decide to pay you a personal visit?'

'Probably—as the Newmans' house is only half a mile or so away.' Stephanie sighed. 'At least *Rosalind* lives only half a mile or so away,' she added. 'I believe Richard moved into an apartment of his own several weeks ago.'

'But you're not sure?'

Stephanie gritted her teeth in frustration with a situation that had already been complicated enough before Rosalind Newman's intervention! 'Look, Jordan, I know how bad this all looks and sounds—especially after what's happened between us the last few days—but—'

'I don't consider the problem you're currently experiencing with Rosalind Newman to have anything to do with what took place between us,' Jordan said.

Stephanie eyed him warily. 'You don't?'

He shrugged. 'You've already assured me that our own relationship only went as far as it did because of your long-held infatuation with Jordan Simpson,' he reminded her coldly. 'Which would seem to indicate that the two incidents have little to do with each other.'

'You were my patient too—'

'I think we can both agree that you never actually got as far as a working relationship with me,' Jordan drawled.

'I didn't have an affair with Richard Newman, either.'

He arched dark brows. 'Did I say that you did?'

'No, but Rosalind did!' Stephanie's cheeks felt warm as she thought of the accusations the other woman had made in front of Jordan.

He gave a shrug as he walked further into the kitchen to perch on the side of one of the stools at the breakfast-bar. 'I think we can safely assume the poor woman has been knocked slightly emotionally off-balance by the breakdown of her marriage.' His mouth tightened. 'So much so that she's looking for someone else to blame.'

Stephanie looked at him uncertainly. 'You really believe me when I say I didn't have an affair with Richard Newman?'

'Shouldn't I?'

Well, of course Jordan should believe her, when it was nothing less than the truth! Stephanie just hadn't expected that he would… 'I do think Rosalind is right about Richard having an affair with someone, though.'

'Just not you?'

She grimaced. 'No.'

Jordan's earlier anger had dissipated in the face of this more pressing problem for Stephanie. Much as he felt sorry for Rosalind Newman's dilemma, her behaviour earlier indicated that she was close to breaking emotionally. Dangerously close.

'Pour us both some coffee, hmm?' Jordan encouraged softly. 'And then you can tell me exactly why you think Newman is having an affair, but has no problem with letting an innocent bystander bear the brunt of his wife's anger.'

'I'm sure you don't need to be bothered with my problems—'

'Having enough of my own, presumably?' Jordan said dryly.

'I didn't mean that!'

'Just pour the coffee, Stephanie, and let me worry about what I do or don't want to be bothered with,' he rasped, and he made himself more comfortable on the bar stool.

Stephanie still looked less than certain, but she poured coffee into two mugs anyway, placing them and milk and sugar on the breakfast bar before sitting on the stool opposite Jordan's.

'What do you want to know?'

'Everything.'

It had all started out innocently enough, as far as Jordan could see. Richard Newman had been involved in a car accident which had resulted in his needing physiotherapy on a daily basis at his home, once he'd been discharged from hospital. Those treatments had lessened to three times a week and begun taking place at Stephanie's small private treatment room once he had regained most of his mobility and returned to work in the City.

'Let me guess,' Jordan commented. 'This is where the trouble started?'

Stephanie gave a heavy sigh. 'It seems that Rosalind and Richard's boss were both still under the impression he was having treatment five afternoons a week.'

'So on those other two afternoons he was meeting someone else?'

'I can only assume he must have been.' Stephanie nodded uncomfortably. 'He certainly wasn't spending them with me.'

'I've already said I believe you, Stephanie,' Jordan said.

She frowned. 'But *why* do you?'

Interesting question, Jordan acknowledged ruefully. Interesting, but totally redundant, since Stephanie had assured him that her only interest in him had been as his actor persona!

'You may have your faults, Stephanie, but I don't believe that dishonesty is one of them,' he said, and he picked up his cane to stand up suddenly. 'I hope this situation works out for you.'

She looked startled. 'You're leaving?'

Jordan gave a hard smile. 'Unless you think we have anything left to say to each other?'

No, Stephanie was pretty sure they didn't have anything left to say that would be in the least conducive to closing the ever-widening gulf that now existed between them. Certainly nothing she could say that would induce

Jordan to stay. To be as in love her as she was with him…

'No,' she said baldly.

'That's what I thought.'

It was better this way, Stephanie assured herself as she accompanied Jordan to the door. No less painful, of course, but at least she had been able to see Jordan again—however briefly. 'Thank you for listening to me,' she said ruefully as she held the door open for him. 'It helped.'

He turned to face her. 'I've made arrangements to fly back to the States tomorrow.'

Stephanie's eyes widened even as she acknowledged the sinking feeling in her chest. 'You have?'

Jordan gave a wry smile. 'I've decided to take your advice and go back to see my original specialist in LA.'

'That's wonderful news!' She smiled warmly.

Jordan's smile was humourless. 'You could try looking a little less pleased to see me go.'

As the woman who was madly in love with him, of course Stephanie wasn't pleased to know that Jordan would be leaving England tomorrow. Going back to his life in LA, to once again be with women like the beautiful Crista Moore.

But as a physiotherapist she couldn't have been more pleased by Jordan's decision to go back to America and seek the professional help she was sure he needed, and which he had totally refused to accept from her or anyone else.

'I'm only pleased because I know you're doing the right thing,' she answered evasively.

'I hope you're right,' he said enigmatically, giving

her one last searching glance before he turned and walked away.

From a professional point of view Stephanie knew she was right.

From a personal one she could feel her heart slowly breaking as she watched Jordan walk away from her for ever…

'Wine! I'm desperately in need of wine!' Joey gasped weakly as she collapsed wearily down onto Stephanie's sofa and put her booted feet up on top of the coffee table.

Stephanie eyed her twin teasingly, before going through to the kitchen to collect up the bottle of red wine and two glasses she had waiting. The two sisters usually spent one evening a week together, catching up on each other's lives. Not that Stephanie had much to tell Joey. The last two weeks had consisted of work, work, and more work. All in a futile effort to block Jordan out of her thoughts by keeping herself busy.

'Tough day?' she wanted to know as she sat down in the chair opposite Joey.

Her sister drank down half the glass of wine before answering her. She was still wearing one of the business suits she always wore to the office, brown today, with a cream silk blouse beneath, her face perfectly made up, her short red hair sleekly styled. 'Just the afternoon. *Bloody* man!' Joey muttered with feeling.

'Which man?' Stephanie couldn't help laughing at her sister's disgruntled expression.

'Gideon St Claire.' Joey glared. 'He has got to be the most pompous, arrogant—'

'*My* Gideon St Claire?' Stephanie echoed sharply as she sat forward tensely.

Joey snorted. 'Well, I wouldn't go *that* far, sis.'

'You know exactly what I mean!' Stephanie was almost beside herself with impatience. 'I didn't think Gideon ever went into a courtroom nowadays?'

'He doesn't—thank God.' Joey gave a shudder at the mere thought of that ever happening. 'He made an appointment and came to see me at my office. I have to say, Stephs, that you have some very powerful friends.' She took another obviously much-needed swig of her wine. 'Gideon St Claire is a seriously scary man. And so damned cold that I'm surprised he doesn't have icicles dripping off him! Still, he did succeed where I failed,' she added grudgingly. 'So he can't be all bad, I suppose...'

'Joey, could you possibly go back a couple of sentences?' Stephanie had finally got over the shock of Joey having met Gideon. 'For one thing, I would hardly call Gideon St Claire a friend of mine—'

'Then maybe he just lusts after you?' her sister dismissed airily. 'Whatever. He got the job done, and that's all that really—'

'Joey, *stop*!' Stephanie silenced her sister sharply, knowing that if Joey was left to her own devices she could go on like this for hours—based purely on her assumption that the person she was talking to should know exactly what she was talking about. Which Stephanie certainly didn't. 'Start from the beginning and tell me exactly *why* Gideon made an appointment and came to see you today.'

Joey took her booted feet off the table to lean forward and refill her glass with red wine. 'It's amazing—the man was only on the case a few days, and he managed to get the whole thing settled without us having to go to court. It was pretty neat, actually,' she added with grudging admiration.

'Joey, I still don't understand a word of what you're saying!' Stephanie wailed frustratedly.

'It's all over, Stephs,' her sister explained patiently. 'With the help of a private investigator, Gideon St Claire has managed to establish that Richard Newman was actually having an affair with his boss's wife. Obviously it's not good news for Rosalind—or Richard Newman, for that matter, considering that he's apparently now lost his job as well as his marriage—but it does mean that you're completely out of the picture,' Joey said warmly. 'All thanks to the arrogant Gideon St Claire.'

Stephanie was reeling with shock. Disbelief. 'But why would he do such a thing?' she finally managed to gasp.

'Because his gorgeous and sexy brother asked him to, of course,' Joey said happily.

'*Jordan* did?'

'Does he have more than one gorgeous and sexy brother?'

'He does, actually,' Stephanie acknowledged faintly, as she thought of the chillingly handsome Lucan St Claire.

'Oh.' Her sister looked nonplussed for a few seconds. But, being the irrepressible Joey, she recovered just as quickly. 'Well, this time it was Jordan Simpson who did the asking.'

Stephanie was still totally stunned. 'Did Gideon tell you that?'

'That and a lot more.' Joey nodded eagerly. 'Apparently Jordan was admitted to a private clinic in LA two weeks ago for yet another operation.'

'Was it successful?' Stephanie was unable to keep the anxiety out of her voice.

'Completely.' Joey took another swig of her wine. 'According to Gideon, the hip joint had become slightly misaligned—I'm sure you understand what that means better than I do,' she added. 'Anyway, the end result is that Jordan Simpson is back up on his two perfectly gorgeous legs. So much so that he has already got backing and is due to play the lead role in the movie of the script he's been writing the last six months.'

It was the best news Stephanie could ever have wished or hoped for. It also explained what Jordan had been doing during those hours when he had disappeared into his study while at Mulberry Hall…

What it *didn't* explain was why Jordan had asked his twin to intercede and help Stephanie in her unwilling involvement with the Newmans' messy divorce—or Gideon St Claire's uncharacteristic gregariousness in discussing his brother so candidly with Joey!

She stood up. 'I don't understand…'

'No?' Joey eyed her knowingly. 'Stephs, exactly how close did you and Jordan get during those few days together in Gloucestershire?'

Stephanie had been fighting against even allowing herself to *think* about Jordan these last couple of weeks, let alone put herself through the torture of remembering the intimacy of their lovemaking. How much she loved him. But this—Jordan asking Gideon to intercede on her behalf in the Newmans' divorce—was so totally unexpected that she no longer knew what to think.

Or to feel.

She needed to talk to Jordan. Needed to know why he had gone to the trouble of asking his brother to help her when there had been so much going on in his own life. Needed to know if Jordan had just been being kind, or if it had been something else that had prompted his actions. What if—?

Stephanie frowned as the doorbell rang.

'Expecting more company?' Joey asked interestedly.

'No,' Stephanie said. 'But at least I know it won't be Rosalind Newman, come to insult me again.'

'Maybe she's come to apologise instead?' Joey suggested ruefully.

'Poor woman.' Stephanie gave a regretful shake of her head before going to answer the door.

Only to be rendered totally speechless when she opened the door and found Jordan standing outside in the hallway. It was too much after what Joey had just told her—a complete overload to Stephanie's already raw emotions. So much so that she instantly burst into loud and choking sobs!

Not quite the reaction he had been hoping for, Jordan acknowledged with a frown as he stepped forward to take the sobbing Stephanie in his arms.

He wasn't really sure what sort of welcome he had been expecting after not seeing or speaking to her for over two weeks, but it certainly hadn't been this!

'Who is it, Stephs? What did you do to her?' An accusing redhead had appeared in the sitting room doorway, frowning darkly as she saw the sobbing Stephanie in Jordan's arms. 'Is it bad news?' She hurried to Stephanie's side. 'What's happened?' she demanded sharply, looking up at Jordan. 'Oh, my God!' Green eyes had gone wide in recognition.

Jordan gave a rueful grin. 'You must be Joey.' Her

facial similarity to Stephanie was obvious, despite the close-cropped hair and formal clothes.

She gave a slightly dazed nod of her head as she continued to stare at him. 'Would you two like to be alone?'

'No!'

'Yes! *Yes*, Stephanie,' Jordan repeated firmly, his arms tightening around her as she would have pulled away. 'It was nice meeting you,' he told Joey warmly over the top of Stephanie's head.

'The pleasure was all mine,' she murmured softly. 'Call me, Stephs.'

She couldn't seem to stop staring at Jordan, even as she gave her sister a perfunctory kiss on the cheek before quietly leaving.

Stephanie felt more than a little foolish over her reaction to seeing him again now that she was alone with him. What on earth must he think of her? Bursting into tears like that just because she had found him standing on her doorstep?

She hastily wiped the evidence of those tears from her cheeks as she straightened. 'What are you doing here, Jordan?' she asked as she pulled away from him. 'I'm not sure you should have flown to England at all when you've only recently undergone surgery,' she added worriedly.

Her breath caught in her throat as she looked at Jordan properly for the first time. His hair was shorter than she remembered, and had been cut in that casually rakish style that only an expensive professional could have achieved. And his face no longer had that grim and strained expression. The lines beside his eyes and mouth seemed to have eased, and his jaw was freshly shaven to reveal that gorgeous cleft in his chin. His eyes were a clear and searching gold as he quizzically returned her gaze. He looked fit and healthy, in a tailored charcoal-coloured jacket over a black shirt and black trousers. And he no longer carried the cane…

'The operation was a success,' Stephanie realised happily.

Jordan's smile widened. 'Yes, it was. Thanks to you,' he added huskily.

She frowned. 'I didn't do anything.'

'You repeatedly told me what a self-pitying idiot I was, and told me to go and get my leg looked at again,' he reminded her dryly. 'Are you going to invite me inside, Stephanie? Or have I made myself so unwelcome you would rather keep me standing out here in the hallway?'

'I—no, of course not.' Stephanie stepped back to allow him to walk into her apartment, her heart lifting as she saw the way Jordan walked only with a slight emphasis on his right leg now—and that was sure to disappear completely, too, after a few more weeks of full mobility.

Except she still had no idea what he was doing here!

She followed him through to the sitting room, the palms of her hands feeling damp as she faced him. 'You told me that Gideon called you a self-pitying idiot too,' she pointed out.

Jordan chuckled softly. 'It somehow had more impact coming from you.'

Stephanie eyed him quizzically. 'I can't imagine why.'

His expression became enigmatic. 'Can't you?'

'No.' God, he looked good, Stephanie acknowledged weakly. Every gorgeous, mesmerising inch of him…

'We'll get to that in a minute,' Jordan said briskly. 'I meant to arrive before Gideon had his meeting with your sister—wanted to explain exactly what was going on before he talked to Joey—but unfortunately my plane was delayed.'

'Yes, what was that all about?' Stephanie frowned. 'Don't get me wrong—it was very kind of you to ask Gideon to help extricate me from any involvement in the Newmans' divorce. I just don't understand why you did it.'

Jordan thrust his hands into his trouser pockets—he still found it a novelty to be able to do even such a simple action without falling flat on his face!—and he looked across at Stephanie through narrowed lids. 'You helped me. I wanted to help you.'

Any hopes that Stephanie might have had concerning Jordan's motives were instantly dashed. Rightly so. What had she expected? That Jordan had helped her because he actually liked her? Loved her? You're living in cloud cuckoo land, Stephanie, she admonished herself derisively.

'I do appreciate it, but you really had no need to put yourself to that trouble on my behalf.'

'I had *every* need, damn it,' Jordan rasped impatiently. 'Rosalind Newman was becoming dangerous. To other people as well as herself. Gideon has talked to her lawyer and advised that she seek medical help before she really does hurt someone.'

'Advised?' Stephanie repeated; she couldn't imagine the coldly arrogant Gideon St Claire doing anything so meek as offering *advice*.

Jordan gave a rueful grimace. 'Okay, so he made it part of the deal—you won't bring any charges against her if she seeks medical help.'

Stephanie gasped. 'But I had no intention of—'

'Could you offer me a coffee or something, Stephanie?' he cut in swiftly. 'It was a long flight, and I came straight here from the airport.'

'I—of course.' What was she thinking of, quizzing Jordan in this way over what had been a very kind act on his part? What did it matter why or how it had been achieved, so long as Stephanie no longer had the cloud of the Newmans' divorce hanging over her head? 'I have coffee already made, but Joey hasn't drunk all the wine if you would prefer that,' she added, as she looked at the half-full bottle on the table. 'I'm afraid Gideon's visit to my sister's office earlier had rather a disturbing effect on her.'

'Gideon has that effect on most people.' Jordan chuckled understandingly. 'And coffee would be great,' he added as he followed Stephanie through to the kitchen, watching her from behind guarded lids as she poured coffee into two mugs.

She looked somewhat thinner than Jordan remembered. There were slight hollows in her cheeks, shadows under those beautiful green eyes, and the stubborn set of her chin seemed more defined. That glorious red-gold hair was drawn back in its usual plait down her spine; a black T-shirt and low-slung fitted jeans outlined her slender curves.

'How have you been, Stephanie?' he asked gruffly as the two of them moved to sit at the breakfast bar.

'Good.' She nodded, her gaze on her coffee mug rather than on him. 'I have lots of work on at the moment, so I'm keeping busy. I hear you're thinking of going back to work again soon, too?' she said lightly.

Jordan wished she would look at him. Allow him to look into the 'windows of her soul' just once, so that he might have at least some idea of how she felt about him being here. 'In a couple of months, yes,' he said. 'Stephanie, I didn't come here to talk about your work or mine.'

Her lashes flickered up and she looked across at him before quickly looking away again. 'I appreciate you taking time from what is no doubt a busy family visit—'

'I came to England specifically to see *you*, Stephanie,' he interrupted. 'I—' He broke off to give an irritated shake of his head as she gave him a startled glance.

Damn it, this had seemed easier when he was sitting in his house in Malibu, just imagining seeing Stephanie again, talking to her. Now that he was actually here with her, within touching distance, Jordan didn't even know where to start!

He stood up to pace the kitchen restlessly as he tried to put into words what he wanted to say. 'Stephanie, if all you have to offer is an infatuation for me as Jordan Simpson, then for as long as it lasts I'll take it.'

Stephanie turned to stare at him in complete confusion. 'I beg your pardon?'

His mouth tightened. 'You were honest enough to tell me that your only reason for being with me, for making love with me at St Claire House, was because you've always had a thing for Jordan Simpson,' he reminded her, a nerve pulsing in his tightly clenched jaw. 'I'm here to tell you that I'm willing to continue a relationship with you on those terms.'

Stephanie's face had gone very pale. 'You want me to have an *affair* with you?'

He frowned fiercely. 'No, damn it. The last thing I want is for you to have an affair with me!'

She blinked at his vehemence. 'But you just said—'

'I just said that I would take that *if* it's all you have to offer,' Jordan corrected.

Stephanie tried to make sense of what Jordan was saying. He *did* want to have an affair with her, but he didn't. What did that mean? 'I don't understand,' she said finally, giving a confused shake of her head.

Jordan glared his frustration. 'It's really quite simple, Stephanie. If I can't have you in my life, then I don't want anyone.'

She looked taken aback. 'I— But you said—'

'I said a lot of things. As did you.' He sighed. 'One of which was a complete misunderstanding on your part. Stephanie, you *didn't* restore my sexual interest— you are the only woman that I want to make love with. Ever.'

Her eyes were wide. 'What about Crista Moore? All those beautiful leggy blondes you usually date?'

His mouth twisted. 'Just two weeks in LA, surrounded by "all those beautiful leggy blondes", was more than long enough for me to know I'm no longer attracted to any of them. The only woman who holds any attraction for me is a certain stubborn redhead who tends to argue with me most of the time.'

She looked shocked. 'You mean *me*?'

'Of *course* you, Stephanie.' He took a deep breath. 'I'm in love with you, damn it!'

'What!' She stared at him disbelievingly.

'You know, I've never said that to a woman in my life before.' Jordan gave a rueful grin. 'I somehow expected that when I did it would be received with a little more enthusiasm! I. Love. You. Stephanie McKinley,' he repeated slowly, so that there should be no further misunderstanding. 'I love you. Jordan St Claire loves you. Jordan Simpson loves you. We all love you. Is that clear enough for you?'

Stephanie was starting to feel light-headed. 'I— But you *can't* love me!'

It was so *not* the reaction that Jordan wanted. '*Why* can't I?'

'Well, because—because I'm just plain ordinary me. And you—well, you're—'

'Jordan Simpson. I know,' he accepted wearily. 'And I'm afraid it's much worse than that, actually. But that's something we can discuss in a few minutes,' he said hollowly. 'Stephanie, I love you, and I very much need to know how you would feel about having a long-term relationship with me. *Very* long-term,' he added firmly.

Stephanie swallowed hard, wondering what could be 'much worse' than him being Jordan Simpson, but too dazed at that moment to care. 'You had your operation because of the things I said about Jordan Simpson, didn't you?' she gasped as the idea suddenly occurred to her. 'Because you didn't think I wanted you as you were?'

'That wasn't the whole reason, no.' He grimaced. 'I obviously couldn't carry on in the way I was. But wanting to be fit and completely well for your sake *did* come into it, yes.'

Stephanie shook her head. 'Jordan, when I left St Claire House—when you came here—I tried to...I felt stupid because of what had happened between us.' She looked up at him emotionally. 'I said those things to you because I thought you had just used me—I was trying to salvage at least some of my pride.'

He looked at her with sudden hope. 'You mean you *aren't* infatuated with Jordan Simpson?'

'Isn't every woman?' Stephanie said as she stood up with a smile.

'Not every one, no,' Jordan retorted. 'Neither do I have any interest in what any other women might think of me.' He reached out to grasp both her hands in his. 'And "just" you isn't plain and ordinary, Stephanie. You're an exceptional woman. Beautiful. Clever. Intelligent. As well as too outspoken for your own good, of course.' He grinned affectionately at her before suddenly sobering. His expression became intense as he looked down at her. 'That time with you in Gloucestershire, and at St Claire House, was more than enough to tell me that you're everything I could ever want in a woman. Everything that I will ever want and always love,' he added fiercely as his hands tightened about hers. 'Stephanie, I don't care if it's Jordan Simpson you're infatuated with. I'll be anyone and anything you want me to be, if only you'll say— Oh, God, you're crying again!' he groaned as the tears began to fall down her cheeks.

'This time I'm crying because I'm happy!' Stephanie assured him emotionally as she looked up at him with glowing eyes. 'I'm not infatuated with Jordan Simpson any more, Jordan. He's been a wonderful object for all my secret fantasies. But it's Jordan St Claire who has occupied my fantasies these past few weeks. Jordan St Claire I fell in love with. Jordan St Claire I made love with at St Claire House.'

'You *love* me?' He looked stunned. 'But I was rude, and bad-tempered, and downright nasty to you a lot of the time. Especially after you told me it was Jordan Simpson you had "a thing" for,' he added darkly.

'I love *you*, Jordan. Whoever you are,' she assured him fervently. 'Rude and bad-tempered. Or magnetic and sexy. It's you I love. *All* of you!' She launched herself into his arms.

Jordan didn't care which of his personas Stephanie loved so long as she continued to kiss him as if she never wanted to stop. These past two weeks in LA without her had told him that he had no desire to live without Stephanie as a permanent part of his life. As the focus of his life!

'Will you marry me, Stephanie?' he asked gruffly, a long, long time later, as the two of them lay naked and replete in each other's arms.

Stephanie glowed up at the man she loved. 'With all my heart, Jordan.'

He chuckled softly. 'Our life together is never going to be dull, is it?'

Their *long* life together, Stephanie hoped, with lots of love and children. 'Are you going to tell me now what the "even worse" is you were referring to earlier?' she asked teasingly.

EPILOGUE

'DOES this mean I have to address you as Lady St Claire from now on?' Joey teased, once Jordan and Stephanie had posed in front of the cameras for the cutting of their wedding cake.

'Stephanie has always been a lady,' Jordan drawled, keeping his arm possessively about his wife's waist.

Stephanie was a very happily dazed lady at the moment!

The last six weeks had been hectic as they'd arranged the wedding in between flying backwards and forwards to LA, as Stephanie had closed down her physiotherapy practice in London and prepared to open it up again in LA when they returned from their honeymoon in a couple of weeks' time.

It had only added to the unreality of it all to learn that Jordan's 'even worse' was that he and Gideon were actually lords, and that Lucan was the Duke of Stourbridge, with Mulberry Hall being his ducal estate.

After their wedding earlier today, *she* was now officially Lady Stephanie St Claire.

Inwardly, she was still just Stephanie. As Jordan was Jordan. All the Jordans. Jordan Simpson. Jordan St Claire. Lord Jordan St Claire. And Stephanie loved every one of them to distraction!

'No, I'm still just Stephs to you,' she assured Joey ruefully, before her sister wandered off with the obvious intention of annoying Gideon as he stood talking with their parents and Molly St Claire.

Stephanie smiled as she looked around the crowded ballroom at St Claire House, where members of her own family and Jordan's mingled happily together.

She turned back to her husband. 'I love you so much, Jordan,' she said quietly to him.

His arms tightened about her. 'I'll love you for ever, Stephanie,' he vowed fiercely.

She moved up on tiptoe to whisper teasingly in his ear. 'Would you like to escape for a personal viewing of my white silk and lace underwear, Lord St Claire?'

Jordan grinned down at her. 'I thought you would never ask, Lady St Claire!'

Yes, for ever with Jordan sounded perfect, as far as Stephanie was concerned…

Coming Next Month

from **Harlequin Presents® EXTRA.** Available April 12, 2011.

#145 PICTURE OF INNOCENCE
Jacqueline Baird
Italian Temptation!

#146 THE PROUD WIFE
Kate Walker
Italian Temptation!

#147 SURF, SEA AND A SEXY STRANGER
Heidi Rice
One Hot Fling

#148 WALK ON THE WILD SIDE
Natalie Anderson
One Hot Fling

Coming Next Month

from **Harlequin Presents®.** Available April 26, 2011.

#2987 JESS'S PROMISE
Lynne Graham
Secretly Pregnant…Conveniently Wed!

#2988 THE RELUCTANT DUKE
Carole Mortimer
The Scandalous St. Claires

#2989 NOT A MARRYING MAN
Miranda Lee

#2990 THE UNCLAIMED BABY
Melanie Milburne
The Sabbatini Brothers

#2991 A BRIDE FOR KOLOVSKY
Carol Marinelli

#2992 THE HIGHEST STAKES OF ALL
Sara Craven
The Untamed

Visit www.HarlequinInsideRomance.com
for more information on upcoming titles!

HPCNM0411

REQUEST YOUR FREE BOOKS!

2 FREE NOVELS PLUS 2 FREE GIFTS!

YES! Please send me 2 FREE Harlequin Presents® novels and my 2 FREE gifts (gifts are worth about $10). After receiving them, if I don't wish to receive any more books, I can return the shipping statement marked "cancel." If I don't cancel, I will receive 6 brand-new novels every month and be billed just $4.05 per book in the U.S. or $4.74 per book in Canada. That's a saving of at least 15% off the cover price! It's quite a bargain! Shipping and handling is just 50¢ per book in the U.S. and 75¢ per book in Canada.* I understand that accepting the 2 free books and gifts places me under no obligation to buy anything. I can always return a shipment and cancel at any time. Even if I never buy another book, the two free books and gifts are mine to keep forever. 106/306 HDN FC55

Name (PLEASE PRINT)

Address Apt. #

City State/Prov. Zip/Postal Code

Signature (if under 18, a parent or guardian must sign)

Mail to the **Reader Service:**
IN U.S.A.: P.O. Box 1867, Buffalo, NY 14240-1867
IN CANADA: P.O. Box 609, Fort Erie, Ontario L2A 5X3

Not valid for current subscribers to Harlequin Presents books.

Are you a current subscriber to Harlequin Presents books and want to receive the larger-print edition?
Call 1-800-873-8635 or visit www.ReaderService.com.

* Terms and prices subject to change without notice. Prices do not include applicable taxes. Sales tax applicable in N.Y. Canadian residents will be charged applicable taxes. Offer not valid in Quebec. This offer is limited to one order per household. All orders subject to credit approval. Credit or debit balances in a customer's account(s) may be offset by any other outstanding balance owed by or to the customer. Please allow 4 to 6 weeks for delivery. Offer available while quantities last.

Your Privacy—The Reader Service is committed to protecting your privacy. Our Privacy Policy is available online at www.ReaderService.com or upon request from the Reader Service.

We make a portion of our mailing list available to reputable third parties that offer products we believe may interest you. If you prefer that we not exchange your name with third parties, or if you wish to clarify or modify your communication preferences, please visit us at www.ReaderService.com/consumerschoice or write to us at Reader Service Preference Service, P.O. Box 9062, Buffalo, NY 14269. Include your complete name and address.

HP11

With an evil force hell-bent on destruction, two enemies must unite to find a truth that turns all-too-personal when passions collide.

Enjoy a sneak peek in Jenna Kernan's next installment in her original TRACKER *series, GHOST STALKER, available in May, only from Harlequin Nocturne.*

"Who are you?" he snarled.

Jessie lifted her chin. "Your better."

His smile was cold. "Such arrogance could only come from a Niyanoka."

She nodded. "Why are you here?"

"I don't know." He glanced about her room. "I asked the birds to take me to a healer."

"And they have done so. Is that *all* you asked?"

"No. To lead them away from my friends." His eyes fluttered and she saw them roll over white.

Jessie straightened, preparing to flee, but he roused himself and mastered the momentary weakness. His eyes snapped open, locking on her.

Her heart hammered as she inched back.

"Lead who away?" she whispered, suddenly afraid of the answer.

"The ghosts. Nagi sent them to attack me so I would bring them to her."

The wolf must be deranged because Nagi did not send ghosts to attack living creatures. He captured the evil ones after their death if they refused to walk the Way of Souls, forcing them to face judgment.

"Her? The healer you seek is also female?"

"Michaela. She's Niyanoka, like you. The last Seer of Souls and Nagi wants her dead."

HNEXP0511

Jessie fell back to her seat on the carpet as the possibility of this ricocheted in her brain. Could it be true?

"Why should I believe you?" But she knew why. His black aura, the part that said he had been touched by death. Only a ghost could do that. But it made no sense.

Why would Nagi hunt one of her people and why would a Skinwalker want to protect her? She had been trained from birth to hate the Skinwalkers, to consider them a threat.

His intent blue eyes pinned her. Jessie felt her mouth go dry as she considered the impossible. Could the trickster be speaking the truth? Great Mystery, what evil was this?

She stared in astonishment. There was only one way to find her answers. But she had never even met a Skinwalker before and so did not even know if they dreamed.

But if he dreamed, she would have her chance to learn the truth.

Look for GHOST STALKER by Jenna Kernan, available May only from Harlequin Nocturne, wherever books and ebooks are sold.

Copyright © 2011 by Jenna Kernan

HNEXP0511

Don't miss an irresistible new trilogy from acclaimed author

SUSAN MEIER

Greek Tycoons become devoted dads!

Coming in April 2011

The Baby Project

Whitney Ross is terrified when she becomes guardian to a tiny baby boy, but everything changes when she meets dashing Darius Andreas, Greek tycoon and now a brand-new daddy!

Second Chance Baby ***(May 2011)***

Baby on the Ranch ***(June 2011)***

www.eHarlequin.com

HR17721

ALWAYS POWERFUL, PASSIONATE AND PROVOCATIVE.

***USA TODAY* BESTSELLING AUTHOR**

MAUREEN CHILD

BRINGS YOU ANOTHER PASSIONATE TALE

KING'S MILLION-DOLLAR SECRET

Rafe King was labeled as the King who didn't know how to love. And even he believed it. That is, until the day he met Katie Charles. The one woman who shows him taking chances in life can reap the best rewards. Even when the odds are stacked against you.

Available May, wherever books are sold.

www.eHarlequin.com

SD73096

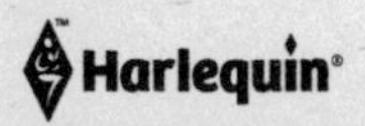

Fan favorite author

TINA LEONARD

is back with
an exciting new miniseries.

Six bachelor brothers are given a challenge—
get married, start a big family and whoever does
so first will inherit the famed Rancho Diablo.
Too bad none of these cowboys is marriage material!

Callahan Cowboys:
Catch one if you can!

The Cowboy's Triplets (May 2011)
The Cowboy's Bonus Baby (July 2011)
The Bull Rider's Twins (Sept 2011)
Bonus Callahan Christmas Novella! (Nov 2011)
His Valentine Triplets (Jan 2012)
Cowboy Sam's Quadruplets (March 2012)
A Callahan Wedding (May 2012)

www.eHarlequin.com

HAR75358

Love Inspired HISTORICAL

INSPIRATIONAL HISTORICAL ROMANCE

Introducing a brand-new heartwarming Amish miniseries,

AMISH BRIDES
of Celery Fields

Beginning in May with

Hannah's Journey

by ANNA SCHMIDT

Levi Harmon, a wealthy circus owner, never expected to find the embodiment of all he wanted in the soft-spoken, plainly dressed woman. And for the Amish widow Hannah Goodloe, to love an outsider was to be shunned. The simple pleasures of family, faith and a place to belong seemed an impossible dream. Unless Levi unlocked his past and opened his heart to God's plan.

Find out if love can conquer all in* HANNAH'S JOURNEY, *available May wherever books are sold.

www.LoveInspiredBooks.com

LIH82868